SALUTE MY SAVAGERY 2

Fumiya Payne

**Lock Down Publications and Ca$h
Presents**
Salute my Savagery 2
A Novel by *Fumiya Payne*

Fumiya Payne

Lock Down Publications
Po Box 944
Stockbridge, Ga 30281

Visit our website @
www.lockdownpublications.com

Copyright 2023 by Fumiya Payne
Salute my Savagery 2

This is a work of fiction. Names, characters, places, and incidents either are products of the author's imagination or are used fictitiously. Any similarity to actual events or locales or persons, living or dead, is entirely coincidental.

Lock Down Publications
Like our page on Facebook: Lock Down Publications @
www.facebook.com/lockdownpublications.ldp
Book interior design by: **Shawn Walker**
Edited by: **Kiera Northington**

Stay Connected with Us!

Text **LOCKDOWN** to 22828 to stay up-to-date with new releases,
sneak peaks, contests and more…
Thank you.

Submission Guideline.

Submit the first three chapters of your completed manuscript to ldpsubmissions@gmail.com, subject line: Your book's title. The manuscript must be in a .doc file and sent as an attachment. Document should be in Times New Roman, double spaced and in size 12 font. Also, provide your synopsis and full contact information. If sending multiple submissions, they must each be in a separate email.

Have a story but no way to send it electronically? You can still submit to LDP/Ca$h Presents. Send in the first three chapters, written or typed, of your completed manuscript to:

LDP: Submissions Dept
Po Box 944
Stockbridge, Ga 30281

DO NOT send original manuscript. Must be a duplicate.

Provide your synopsis and a cover letter containing your full contact information.

Thanks for considering LDP and Ca$h Presents.

ACKNOWLEDGEMENTS...

All praise to the Most High. Because not only has He allowed my journey to continue, but He enables me to write what I hope is enjoyable entertainment. (Explicit, but tasteful.)

Ca$h... again, gratitude for the opportunity. And a double salute to the exceptional level of patience with which you deal with me. Because I think it's safe to say anybody else would've been dropped me off.

If you're loyal at heart and a king by deed, then I pray you prevail against all opposition.

To my beautiful sisters of the struggle... I love y'all with my whole entire heart. I am a product of pain, so I know the difficulty in sometimes finding the strength to continue stepping. But have we not borne witness to women who've turned raindrops into rainbows? And remember, ain't no story without struggle!

Fumiya Payne

Chapter 1

Wearing gas masks and latex gloves, two people were perched on opposite sides of a kitchen table, dipping red capsules into a mixing bowl brimming with a powdery substance. Once capped, they tossed it into a growing pile and reached for another empty capsule. Also within their reach were two Glocks 30's and a bucket of acid.

After filling over a thousand capsules, which were raked into several Ziploc bags and placed inside a backpack, they began cleansing the kitchen of every wrongdoing crumb.

Staring in satisfaction at their sanitation, one of the men slipped the backpack over his shoulder and they exited the kitchen.

Dutifully settled on a couch in the living room was Double-O, who had a mini assault rifle lying across his lap. On the coffee table before him was a laptop that showed an outside view of the apartment's parameter.

"What up, y'all good?" he asked as the two people were removing their masks.

"Bro, not only is this nigga a fucking chef." King smiled as he draped an arm around his light-skinned accomplice. "But the nigga got vision, you hear me?"

An exceptional chemist, despite being barely old enough to legally purchase alcohol, Smurf had recently quadrupled the single brick of Fentanyl. Using several secretive ingredients, his main addition had been heroin. Because not only did it provide the drug with a lasting high, but it would instill the withdrawal effects that created addiction.

And as part of a marketing strategy, he'd chosen the red capsules on account of their ability to stand out. So, with the potency of their product surely surpassing all competition, it wouldn't be long before every addict in the city was in search of the brightly-colored capsules.

King sent out a brief text, from which he received a response ten minutes later.

"Come on, we out," he said upon reading the two-worded reply.

With Double-O holding the rifle in plain sight, the trio attentively marched from the newly leased apartment to either side of a Dodge Durango.

Stationed behind the wheel was Unique, who wore designer shades and a hooded tracksuit. She leaned over to kiss King's lips as he settled across from her in the passenger seat. "You ready, bae?" she huskily breathed into his mouth.

"Am I?" he emphatically answered. "Girl, I been waiting on this moment for a minute."

To help expedite the expansion of his clientele, Unique had convinced King to go along with a bold move, one that could possibly result in a deadly backlash.

Unique was on the verge of backing out, when a car suddenly sped up and blocked her in.

Turning to stare in surprise at the purple Hellcat, King and Double-O exchanged a puzzled look. *How the fuck she know where we at?* They both wondered.

Puma exited the car and came around to its passenger side, where she leaned against the door and crossed her arms. It was a subtle gesture, but the crossing of her arms was meant to signify a peaceful intrusion. At least for the moment.

Also forsaking their firearms, King and Double-O hopped out and headed in her direction.

"What's good?" King awkwardly smiled under Puma's piercing stare. "I see you and bro ain't been answering y'all phones."

Double-O cut his eyes at King in irritation. Considering the ink from his signature on the lease had barely dried, King should've adopted a more aggressive approach.

Puma smirked, then rose up off the car. "What you got going on, King?"

Before he could answer, Double-O intervened. "What's up, Puma, everything good?"

"Shit, I don't know, you tell me. Because my energy ain't changed. But you niggas been acting weird as fuck." Her observant eyes had also noticed neither man was wearing their N.F.L. chain, something they once slept in.

Double-O shook his head. "Nah, niggas just got tired of standing by the edge of the table, waiting for the scraps to fall, you feel me? So, we decided to put food on our own plate. But ain't a ounce of love lost. And if ever y'all need our assistance, we just a phone call away."

"That's what's up." Puma nodded, thinking how unfortunate it was that two boys she once saw as siblings would soon become meals on Martha's menu, along with the weasel behind the wheel.

As Puma turned to walk off, King called out, "What's up with bro, is he good?"

She paused to peer over the hood. "Focus on that plate and let me worry about the rest."

As they watched Puma pull off, Double-O growled at King through gritted teeth, "Nigga, don't ever tuck your tail like that again. I don't give a fuck if she got bodies. Nigga, I got more bodies. And you know what else I got?"

"What?"

"Your back. So, unless you standing before the Most High on Judgement Day, then you ain't gotta bite your tongue for nobody."

***

As Unique was parallel parking in front of a cellphone store on the west side, the Durango was being closely observed by several young hooligans who were undoubtedly harboring handguns beneath their dark hoodies. The larcenous twinkle in their beady eyes was suggestive of their motive for loitering outside the store, they were on the lookout for an easy, but lucrative lick.

Advising King to stay alert while accompanying Unique into the store, Double-O lowered his window and locked eyes with the cruelest-looking crook of the crew. The message in his unblinking stare was clear and concise, try and die.

With a weapon wedged in his waistband as he walked behind Unique, King openly offered each man eye contact.

"Y'all rather rob a bank," he casually cautioned them before entering the store.

Inside the small establishment, which was presently empty of customers, Unique was greeted by a middle-aged Arab who was planted behind the display counter.

"Well, well, well!" he cheerfully beamed, "look who finally decided to drop in."

"Hey, Muhammad." Unique smiled, reaching out to shake the hand of her former phone provider.

"How have you been?" he genuinely inquired. Housing a secret fetish for chocolate, Muhammad had always had an eye for Unique's pretty face and voluptuous frame. But the opportunity for a business proposal had just never presented itself.

"I can't complain." She shrugged. "You know, just taking the bitter with the sweet."

"Well, this obviously isn't a social call," he said, casting a quick glance in King's direction. "So, how can I be of service?"

As King edged away to inspect the assortment of phones, Unique placed a piece of paper on the counter and quietly requested, "I need you to transfer this number to another phone line.

Muhammad wore a thoughtful expression while eyeing the piece of paper. Coupled with personal experience and King's presence, he had a pretty good idea of what their intentions were.

Unique extracted an envelope from her handbag and extended it to Muhammad. "Five grand for something that'll take less than five minutes. And you have my word it won't come back to you."

"But I can't guarantee how long it'll last," he warned before accepting the money. "Because they can easily have it switched back."

Unique cunningly smiled. "We won't need long at all."

After disappearing into a back room for several minutes, Muhammad returned to inform her the line had been transferred.

"Thank you so much, Muhammad," Unique stated, as she patted a hand of gratitude over her heart. "This a favor I won't soon forget."

She and King were barely out of the store, when his phone began vibrating. "What up doe?" he answered.

While listening to the caller, he slipped a slight nod to the three knuckleheads, who had wisely decided to stand down.

"A'ight, meet me at the Walgreen's on 6-Mile," King instructed before disconnecting the call.

Cheesing from ear-to-ear as he draped an arm around Unique, King kissed her cheek and exclaimed, "With a woman like you, I can't lose!"

The volume of calls King received while en route to Walgreen's was unbelievable. The ceaseless ringing was the result of forwarding a phone number that belonged to a drug dealer who was already established. While he'd likely realize something was wrong within an hour or two, that was more than enough time for King to execute the final part of the plan.

When Unique wheeled into the Walgreen's parking lot, there was a countless number of cars idling in wait. It's as if the store announced they were having a free clearance sale.

"Remember," King said, while passing Double-O and Smurf a Ziploc bag apiece, "give 'em my new number and double."

To lure in the loyalty of every addict in attendance, King and his team would prey on their greed by generously providing them with double the amount of what they were purchasing. The consumption of so many capsules would ultimately lead to an overdose, or a newfound addiction to Fentanyl. Either way, King and his team would soon seize a sizeable slice of the city's drug trade, a reward for which they agreed was worthy of war.

With King taking endless calls while hurrying from car to car, he approached the passenger side of a pickup truck and greeted its driver through the lowered window. "What up doe?"

"Yeah, let me get a gram," he said, nervously peering around the parking lot.

When King dropped a handful of capsules into his palm, the man frowned, "What the fuck is this?"

"Way more than what you bought, and twice as strong. So be careful."

"Oh, and by the way," King added before racing off to the next customer, "write down our new number. The feds on that old one."

By the time they serviced the last car, King had already directed another wave of addicts to a nearby location.

As they hopped back inside the Durango, King excitedly turned in his seat. "Nigga, didn't I tell y'all we'd have a million by March! From now on, if I tell you a duck can pull a truck, then shut the fuck up and hook it up!"

Allowing King to bask in the glory of her game plan's success, Unique flashed a subtle sneer as she steered them to the next destination.

This shit too easy, she smiled to herself. *Like selling pussy to a prisoner.*

Chapter 2

Puma pulled into a housing project and parked adjacent to a white sedan. Unfolding himself from the Audi's leather interior was Dolphin, who came around the car and joined her inside the Hellcat.

"What's good?" he greeted, extending his fist for a pound.

"Revenge," Puma honestly answered. "Because I swear, I can't sleep till I get it, you feel me?"

Dolphin nodded in understanding, as he also had an appetite for a similar dish. Dolphin removed a loaf of money from within his Gucci windbreaker. "I know shit crazy right now," he said, handing Puma the remainder of what was owed from the first shipment. "But I was just wondering if you gon' be able to keep the boat afloat. Because at the rate we sailing, I'ma be on dry land in like a week or two."

Knowing he was referring to the dwindling of his drug supply, Puma's mind first flashed back to the promise she'd made him on the day they met, then to the disheartening trip to the dealership in Dearborn. While she usually succeeded in standing behind her word, this was an instance when she may have bitten off more than she could chew. Because it's not every day you encountered a connect who had more bricks than a construction company.

"I ain't even gon' lie to you, my baby," she said in admittance. "The way it's looking, shit probably gon' get worse before it get better. So, I don't blame you if you want to explore other options. Because I know you got mouths to feed."

"Them facts," Dolphin nodded. "But like I said, it'll be a week or two before it dry up. And even then, I'm still ten toes. Because when a nigga was on the verge of starving, you fed me. So, I can't just act like that ain't never happen, you feel me? And besides, I got faith you gon' figure it out."

Impressed by his level of loyalty, which she would've banked on King and Double-O having, Puma reached out to firmly grip Dolphin's hand. "I appreciate that, brodie. And unless a nigga put me to bed, then I'ma most definitely do everything I can to keep this bitch afloat. Because it's sink or swim... and I'll be damned if we drown."

As Puma drove off and Dolphin reentered the Audi, his right-hand, Nooni, had a fierce grip on the wheel as he clenched his jaw in anger.

Dolphin frowned in concern. "What's good, my baby?"

Shaking his head, Nooni answered in a seething tone, "It's like when it rain, it pours, bro."

While Dolphin had been in the car with Puma, Nooni received a call from one of their most gainful workers. Partially informing Nooni of a theft that could cost them a fortune, he wisely refrained from freely speaking and suggested they link up ASAP. "...Because we gotta serious problem, bro."

As a Chevy Traverse turned into the projects, Dolphin and Nooni exited the Audi.

In hustling attire, a hooded sweat suit and white Forces, the worker, named Finesse, emerged from the SUV's passenger seat.

"What's popping?" he solemnly greeted, exchanging firm shakes with both men.

"Shit, what's good?" Dolphin replied in an inquisitive tone.

"Yo, I swear to god, bro, it's like, one minute this bitch was pinging nonstop," he said in reference to the phone in his hand, "Then the next minute this bitch just stopped ringing."

After Kavoni had instructed Dolphin to convert their drug sales from trap houses to cellphones, he appointed Finesse as his primary "phone handler." With a gluttonous appetite and a nun's honesty, Dolphin trusted the young hustler to haul in a daily five grand or better. And true enough, Finesse had not only met his expectations, but would often surpass them.

"After a half-hour, I knew something was wrong," Finesse continued. "So, me knowing the game, I shot straight to the closest Arab store. And I found out somebody forwarded the number to another line."

Dolphin looked at Nooni and smirked. First someone had robbed and killed the man he viewed as a father figure. And now someone had been bold enough to actually remove food from his plate. Although he wasn't a gambling man, Dolphin would've wagered every dollar in his daughter's trust fund both incidents were tied to the same people.

And he'd be a winner.

"Alright, listen, I just need you to sit tight," Dolphin calmly counseled. "Because it's only a matter of time before one of them junkies reach out. Now, they gon' definitely be looking for something in return, and you just make sure to give it to 'em. Because trust me, they gon' be the one to lead us in the right direction, you feel me?"

Nodding his head at the wisdom of Dolphin's thinking, Finesse grinned. "I feel you, my baby."

While watching the SUV exit the parking lot, Dolphin addressed Nooni without turning. "Yo, when we find out who these niggas is, we gon' have to set an example that'll make *CNN!*"

Fumiya Payne

Chapter 3

When Puma arrived at her residence later that evening, she took notice of an aqua-blue Impala parked across the street. Through its light tint, she saw the silhouette of someone behind the wheel. Turning into her driveway, Puma withdrew Martha from her waistband, then exited the car and boldly marched in the Impala's direction. With the weapon shielded behind her right leg, her finger was curled over the trigger, pleading to squeeze off all twenty-three.

Jazz emerged from the car as Puma was crossing the street.

"So, this what a bitch gotta do to see you?" she asked with an obvious attitude. "Camp all out in front of your shit?"

Since they made the disturbing discovery of Kavoni's blood and N.F.L. chain inside that garage, Puma hadn't answered or returned any of Jazz's calls. While part of it was due to being mentally drained and emotionally withdrawn, the majority resulted from distrustful thoughts.

"Right now ain't the time," Puma replied as she slyly slid Martha in the small of her back.

"How is it not?" Jazz demanded. "When I haven't seen or heard from you in over a whole week. You treating me like I'm a fucking outsider or something. Like—"

As a certain thought suddenly dawned on Jazz, she narrowed her eyes at Puma and asked, "You think I might've had something to do with that shit, don't you?"

"I really don't know what to think." Puma shrugged. But in all actuality, she was definitely convinced Unique was involved. Because everything was running smoothly until she entered the picture. And the fact that it was Jazz who made the introduction, it would be naive of Puma to exclude her as a possible perpetrator in Kavoni's kidnapping.

Slowly shaking her head in disbelief, Jazz replied, "I can't believe you would think I'd betray you like that. Like I haven't risked my life and freedom for you. On multiple occasions."

Fumiya Payne

"Man, niggas take the stand on their own brothers," Puma fired back. "So don't try to act like shit ain't foul out here. Like mu'fuckas ain't doing whatever to get ahead."

As the two women were holding one another's stare, Puma broke eye contact to casually scan the area. Checking for a pair of pupils possibly peeking from behind curtains, she was seriously considering shutting off Jazz's electricity. But as wisdom prevailed, she decided to address the matter at a later date.

"Look, it ain't no mystery I got feelings for you," Puma said in an attempt to ease the tension. "And I definitely appreciate everything you've done for me. But right now, girl, my head all fucked up. It's like I don't know whether I'm going or coming. So just give me some time to figure it out."

Jazz scoffed in response. "Yeah, I guess that explains why some bitch keep looking out your fucking window. She helping you figure shit out."

Puma glanced toward the house, then before she was given a chance to reply, Jazz jumped back in her car and sped off.

After a moment of thoughtfully watching the car's receding taillights, Puma turned to walk back to the Hellcat, where she fetched several bags of fast food.

Upon entering the house, she was greeted by an energetic Squeeze, whose excitement heightened at the scents wafting from within the Wendy's bags.

"Man, back your greedy ass up!" she playfully pushed him. "This ain't for you."

Seated on a white sofa, with one of her legs tucked beneath her, Shawna observed them with a subtle smile.

"What you watching?" Puma smiled as she entered the living room, with Squeeze hugging her heels.

"Just some show on *MTV*," she quietly answered.

As Puma joined Shawna on the couch and began removing food from the bags, Squeeze instantly assumed a seated position. Fully aware of what was in store, he licked his greedy lips in anticipation.

"Let me get this hungry-ass nigga out the way," she laughed, unwrapping several sandwiches.

20

Once she and Shawna had finished eating and given their scraps to Squeeze, Puma turned to face the fourteen-year-old with a solemn expression.

"I don't want you to take this the wrong way," she began in a soft tone, "but I think it would be best if you lived somewhere else. Because it's a lot going on right now, and I can't honestly say you wouldn't be in danger. So, before your blood end up on my hands, I'd just rather see you in a more stable environment."

Shawna lowered her head before quietly asking, "Is it because I turned on the TV without your permission?"

"Of course not," Puma assured her as she quickly slid closer to lay a comforting hand on Shawna's forearm. "Girl, you welcome to anything in this house. But it would really mess me up if something was to happen to you on account of me. Especially if it could've been prevented. I'm just going through some shit right now, Shawna. And I really don't know what's gon' happen to me."

Although Puma didn't presently have a plan, she did have every intention on annihilating the four culprits she believed to be responsible for her best friend's demise. And because such a volume of violence would require a vigilant mindset, she preferred to have zero distractions and only one commitment, genocide.

***

"You got my number," Puma said to Shawna as they were parked outside of her grandmother's house. "So, if there's anything you ever need, then don't hesitate to call. I don't care if it's one in the morning."

With her head down and eyes focused on the floorboard, Shawna slowly nodded.

Puma removed a roll of money from her pocket and held it out for Shawna to take. "This should at least hold you down for a month. But if not, just hit me up."

Softly stating words of gratitude, Shawna hid the money in her backpack, which contained clothing and toiletries Puma had recently purchased.

"And I'm serious, Shawna," Puma reiterated. "If ever there's something you need, I expect to be the first person you call. I might not be stable right now, but I still got your back.''

Shawna turned away and raised an arm to erase the footsteps of her falling tears.

Puma latched on to her arm in concern. "Shawna, what's wrong?

"Nothing," she sniffled, grasping the door handle. "I'll be alright."

The victim of traumatic experiences that would break the spirits of the average adolescent girl, Shawna had grown accustomed to her silent cries going unheard.

Pulling her arm free of Puma's hold, she exited the car and trudged toward her grandmother's screened-in porch.

When the front door was opened by an older black lady, Shawna turned to look back at Puma before entering the darkened house.

As Puma tapped the horn twice and slowly pulled off, there was a strong sense of concern she was unable to ignore. She tried to convince herself that surely the girl was in good hands with her Nana. But what would cause her to suddenly break down in tears? It felt as if Shawna dreaded the living arrangement, though she had called in advance to inform her grandmother of her arrival. But because Puma had made it a point not to inquire about Shawna's background, so as to avoid forming an attachment, there could definitely be more to the story than what she assumed.

Recalling the countless nights, she had prayed for God to either take away the pain or her breath, Puma found herself making a U-turn in traffic. For her journey couldn't continue until she knew with certainty that Shawna was in a safe habitat.

Puma parked back in front of the small house and first tried to reach Shawna on the phone she'd bought her earlier that morning. When she didn't pick up after the second attempt, Puma exited the car.

Ascending the front porch, Puma was on the verge of knocking, when she heard a woman's voice bellowing from inside.

"...Because I'm telling you right now, Shawna, I will fuck your ass up, girl. So don't play with me. And you not gon' lay up in here, thinking you gon' eat up all my got-damn food, either. The first time I catch your fat ass—"

Sickened to her stomach, Puma ignored the doorbell and banged on the front door like an officer from the Detroit Police Department.

"Who is it?" the grandmother shouted.

In response, Puma banged again.

Angrily brushing aside a curtain, the woman snatched the front door open, and demanded to know why Puma was knocking like someone inside owed her money.

Puma stared past the woman and into the living room, where Shawna was timidly seated on a plaid couch. Upon looking up to see Puma, there was a flash of hope and relief in her teary eyes.

Ignoring the woman's inquiries, Puma summoned Shawna with a wave of the hand. "Come on, girl, let's get up out of here."

The grandmother turned to growl at her granddaughter, "Bitch, if you don't sit your ugly ass down, I'ma knock the fuck out of you."

Puma moved to step further into the house and the woman grabbed her arm in obstruction. "Don't make me call the police on your lil' manly ass. So, you better gon' and get up out of here."

Eyeing the woman's hand as if was plagued with leprosy, Puma jerked her arm free and hissed through clenched teeth, "Lady, I'll kill you just as easily as I would a roach. Now back the fuck up."

Consumed with fear from the detection of deadliness in Puma's demeanor, the woman took a step back and yelled for her son's presence and protection. "Aye, Anthony!"

In turn, Puma yelled out, "Aye, Martha!" and withdrew the Glock from the small of her back.

Her mouth agape at the sight of the full-size semi, the woman warned her son to stay back as he came racing from upstairs.

"You better listen to her," Puma advised the herculean as she racked a round into the gun's chamber. "Cause all them muscles ain't no match for Martha. She'll deflate that lil' shit in a heartbeat."

While holding both targets at bay, Puma approached Shawna and extended her hand in invitation. She hesitated for only a split second, before grabbing her backpack in one hand and Puma's palm in the other.

As Puma escorted her out the front door, she paused on the porch to peer back at the woman. "Remember what I said about that roach. Because the same way I feel today is the same way I'll feel forever."

Inside the car, Puma was bringing the engine to life, when Shawna unexpectedly leaned over to grip her in a fierce hug. This was the first time in her life that someone had come to her aid, and she was overwhelmed with emotions. So regardless of what lay ahead, this was a moment she'd forever cherish.

Touched by the girl's affectionate display, Puma reciprocated the gesture by squeezing her back. And though she lacked the ability to foresee what the future held, she inwardly vowed to shelter Shawna from further suffering.

"As long as I got oxygen in my body," she whispered into her ear, "I'll make sure no one ever mistreats you again. And that's a promise I'll keep with my life.''

Chapter 4

Wearing only a gold choker flooded with dancing diamonds, Unique was surrounded by stacks of money as she sat Indian style in the center of a large bed. Filled with a euphoric feeling from being in the presence of nearly two hundred grand, she carefully recounted the money for the second time.

Since slyly convincing King to appoint her as his personal accountant, Unique was in awe of how rapidly they were rising up the rungs of riches. With several people working the "drug phones," it had been only a few weeks since their arrival into the game and they'd already made more money than dealers who had been doing it for decades.

Upon completion of her second count, she grabbed a handful of bills and crawled to the edge of the bed.

Settled on the floor, with his eyes glued to the TV and his thumbs darting over a controller, King was engrossed in the *Modern Warfare* edition of *Call of Duty*.

When Unique began drizzling bills over the crown of his head, he looked up and was surprisingly met with the hardened nipples of her dangling breasts.

"Oh yeah?" He smiled. "That's how you feeling up there?"

"I'm saying, you gon' keep playing that silly game, or you gon' come up and celebrate with me and my girl?"

"Your girl?" He frowned as if he was in sole ownership of her yoni.

"Yeah, you heard me," she said before lying back and spreading her legs. "So, if you don't like what I said, then come do something about it."

Peeling off his clothes to expose a semi-hard erection, King climbed on the bed and dove head-first into her heated pool.

With a fistful of his dreads, Unique hissed like a venomous snake as he used his tongue to tattoo his name over her clitoris.

"Whose girl you say this was?" King looked up, his mouth glistening with juices from her leaking yoni.

Panting like a dehydrated dog, Unique pleaded for him to finish inscribing his name.

He teasingly tickled his tongue over her throbbing clitoris before repeating, "Whose girl did you say this was?"

Desperate for the release of the mounting pressure between her thighs, she catered to his ego and exclaimed, "It's yours!"

"A'ight, then," he cockily replied before resuming his tattoo work.

Her legs quivering, Unique was on the verge of coming, when she suddenly pushed his head away and instructed him to lay on his back. As soon as he complied, she straddled his face, got a firm grip on the headboard and began grinding her yoni into his opened mouth.

"I'm 'bout to come! I'm 'bout to come!" she repeatedly screamed as her eyes rolled upwards and her body convulsed as if being struck by jolts of electricity.

After flooding his mouth with more cream than he could consume, she crawled forward and placed herself in a deeply arched doggystyle position.

"Come get it, daddy," she moaned into the sheet.

Using the back of his hand to wipe his mouth, King aligned himself with her opening and plunged straight to its base.

Taken by surprise, her eyes widened right before she released a piercing scream.

With his claws clutching each side of her waist, he crushed her with forceful strokes that sent provocative ripples through her soft cheeks.

Her breathing irregular, Unique was speaking in tongues in between pleasurable sobs. She was presently grateful for having had the patience to teach him how to properly please her.

Ready to bring their session to a close, she reached back to halt his movements. "Be still and let me take you for a ride, daddy."

Using the strength of her vaginal muscles to place his pole in a chokehold, she looked over her shoulder and began winding her backend in various directions. Circling, pulling, pushing.

"I'm ready for that nut, daddy!" she pled before picking up the pace. As she was slamming herself back and forth into his pelvis, saturating his stomach and stem with her sticky substance, she felt him swell up inside her and quickly unhitched herself. She turned and presented her face as his canvas, something she'd never done.

"Let me taste it," she said, fully extending her long tongue.

As his heartbeat accelerated in disbelief and excitement, he loudly groaned while painting her face with spurting jets of thick semen.

"Gottt-dammn, girl," he breathlessly smiled before collapsing onto the bed. "You gon' fuck around and make a nigga put a ring on that lil' shit."

"Yeah, you just better make sure it's a big one," she said, climbing out of bed. "Cause you ain't gon' never find another bitch to do it on and off the court like me."

In total agreement, King lustfully watched the enticing jiggle of her chocolate cheeks as she stumbled off to the bathroom.

Carrying a warm washcloth, Unique returned minutes later and gently cleaned King's lower half.

With his hands clasped behind his head, and a thrilling feeling in his heart, he proudly grinned down at the woman with whom he hoped to spend the remainder of his life.

Unique looked up to return his smile, her mind entertaining entirely different thoughts. Sinister thoughts King wouldn't believe she was capable of conceiving.

As they were lying in bed, with her head on his chest, she suddenly spoke without looking up. "Daddy, I'm lightweight worried."

"About what?" he immediately inquired.

She purposely hesitated before answering, "About Puma."

While King didn't respond, he too was harboring the same concerning thought. For he could sense that something had happened with Kavoni and she was holding him responsible. well aware of the level of love she retained for his brother, he could only imagine the wrath she'd impose upon all parties she assumed guilty.

"I cherish you more than life, King," Unique continued. "And I don't want anything to jeopardize our relationship. Because I honestly don't know what I'd do if you wasn't a part of my life. I let you get closer to me than any other man, and the thought of losing you scares me."

With her words mirroring his own inner thoughts, he tilted her face upwards and solemnly stated, "On my dead mama, I'll murder anyone who gets in our way. I just need you to continue holding me down."

Adding additional wood to the fire, Unique warned, "But, daddy, you gotta be careful. Because I remember you saying how active Puma is in them streets.''

As predicted, her statement caused him to redden in anger.

"What, you think I can't get her clapped?" he said, springing up from the bed. "My nigga Double-O will box anything I tell him to."

Inwardly smiling, Unique replied, "Just calm down, daddy. I didn't mean it like that."

"Nah," he said, shaking his head. "You think I'm pussy, or something."

"Not at all. I just want you to start thinking more like a boss. Because you in a different tax bracket now. So, you can't never let pride rob you of your accomplishments, you feel me?"

"So, what the fuck you suggesting?"

"I'm suggesting that you should take advantage of all the pieces on your board. Because what's the point of having pawns if you ain't pushing 'em. And it ain't that you less dangerous, it's more about playing your role as the king, which means keeping yourself safe by all means. Because in the end, it's just gon' be me and you."

King could only nod his head in agreement. He never thought in a million years he'd be blessed with someone as beautiful and bold as Unique. One who was the true definition of a ''ride-or-die.''

Rejoining her in bed, King assured her that he'd take her counsel to heart. "I know you just want the best for me, love. And I appreciate you more than I can tell you with words. And trust me, I'm not gon' let nobody fuck up what we got going. I waited too long to meet a woman like you to just let you go."

Although he had yet to voice it, King had fallen hopelessly in love with Unique. For her, there wasn't a bridge he wouldn't burn or a murder he wouldn't sanction. He honestly believed she was capable of providing him with the type of mother's love for which he had always yearned.

But if only he knew...

Fumiya Payne

Chapter 5

Carrying a slew of shopping bags, Puma and Shawna exchanged light conversation as they exited the mall. After spending nearly three hours and five grand in various stores, they agreed their next stop should be at the closest restaurant.

"Girl, you gon' be fly as hell when you step up in that school.'' Puma smiled as they were loading the bags in the trunk of her car. "Them lil' bitches gon' be hating like a mu'fucka."

Puma may not have been the most suitable guardian by society's standards, but she did know the importance of keeping Shawna in school. So, in an effort to enliven the experience, Puma had ensured that her appearance would be up to par. In fact, she had another surprise that would surely blow the girl's mind.

After appeasing their appetites at Popeye's Chicken, Puma informed Shawna that she needed to make one last stop before they headed home.

Pulling into the parking lot of a jewelry store, she asked Shawna if she'd accompany her inside. "I might need your opinion on something."

Inside the establishment, a middle-aged woman was standing behind the counter as they approached it.

"Hi, how may I help you lovely ladies?" She plastered on a smile as fake as her uplifted bosom.

"My name's Shy'Ann Richardson, and I'm here to pick up my necklace."

"Oh, yes!'' she exclaimed in remembrance of the name, "We've been expecting you."

After requesting and carefully expecting Puma's identification, the woman presented her with a pink jewelry case.

Puma opened it to reveal a gold necklace by David Yurman. Attached to it was a letter "S" pendant sprinkled with small, sparkling diamonds.

"So, what you think?'' she asked Shawna, holding it up.

"I think it's beautiful," she truthfully admitted.

"That's good," Puma said, reaching out to clasp it around Shawna's neck. "Because it's yours."

Her eyes widening as she emitted an audible gasp, Shawna's mouth went slack in surprise. She just knew this day was a dream from which she'd soon awaken.

As they were leaving the store, Puma noticed a troubled expression on Shawna's face.

"What up, girl, you good?" she inquired once they had reentered the car. She'd thought the number of gifts would've uplifted the girl's spirits.

In answer, a set of tears trickled down Shawna's cheeks.

But before Puma could panic, she softly spoke, "It just feel like I'm dreaming. 'Cause ain't nobody never did nothing nice for me in my whole life.'' She looked up at Puma with a tearful expression. "I don't want you to think I'm ungrateful. Because I'm not. But I guess I just don't really know how to respond. I'm sorry, Puma."

Before Puma's timely intervention, Shawna had been considering suicide as her only means of escape. The physical, mental, and emotional pain was too great for her alone to bear. Without a listening ear or a helping hand, she saw death as her best option. Her only option. And it wasn't as if anyone would be heartbroken by her absence. Then, as she was building the courage for her earthly departure, a guardian angel suddenly appeared, offering a sense of hope and deliverance.

Deeply touched by the raw sentiment of Shawna's statement, Puma pulled the girl into her arms. "You're a beautiful baby, Shawna. Both inside and out. And just because you've had a rough life doesn't mean you don't deserve better. It just means your time hasn't come yet. But it will. So don't ever give up. No matter how hard it gets. And always remember, no good story lacks a struggle."

From a lengthy conversation they recently had, Puma knew Shawna's mother died from a drug overdose when she was just a small child. Initially taken in by a grandmother who condemned her for being overweight, she was constantly subjected to ridicule and physical abuse.

Eventually given to her drug-addicted aunt, she would become a victim to the same villain who had violated Puma. Needless to say, the first fourteen years of Shawna's life had been an experience no child should ever encounter.

"Thank you so much for everything, Puma," Shawna stated in a sincere tone. "You the nicest person I ever met. And I promise I'm not gon' ever take off this necklace."

As they were driving home, Puma couldn't help but feel a mixture of emotions. She was joyful at having a positive effect on Shawna's life but riddled with guilt by the attachment she knew the girl was forming. Because it's no secret her lifestyle lessened her chances of celebrating her next birthday. And if something happened to her, then what would become of Shawna?

Puma decided her only option was to ensure the girl was financially secure should her soul get snatched. So, before she turned down the road of revenge, she'd first take a look into King's new net worth. And just maybe she and Martha could kill two birds with one bullet.

***

Lying under the warmth of her comforter, Puma was awakened from her sleep by a faint noise. Slowly sliding her hand beneath the pillow, she grabbed Martha and listened closely for the sound of nearby footsteps.

Once certain she was alone in the bedroom, she quietly slipped from within the covers and crept toward the door, which she cracked open and listened. She involuntarily jumped at a muffled sound that came from downstairs. Someone was in her house.

Instinctively sensing it was an intruder and not Shawna, she backpedaled to her closet and exchanged Martha for a fully auto AK-47. Quietly as possible, she racked a blue-tipped cartridge into its chamber. Wielding the weapon in both hands, she cautiously advanced out into the hallway. Her instincts proved to be on point as she peered in Shawna's room and took in her curled-up form beneath the blanket.

With her finger grazing the trigger in preparation, Puma descended the staircase with the stealth of a Navy Seal. Mindful of the likelihood that there were multiple intruders, she swiveled the "Chopper" from left-to-right in search of a moving target. She now realized she had exposed her hand to King and Double-O too soon, and now it was possible her elementary mistake could be the cause of her demise.

Reaching the bottom landing, her heartbeat quickened at what sounded like a muffled voice coming from the living room. Her back against the wall, Puma tightened her grip on the rifle, took a deep breath and pivoted in the direction of the voice. When the male intruder turned around at the feel of her presence, Puma stopped breathing as her eyes enlarged in utter disbelief.

Chapter 7

Flashback...

After declaring himself the devil's offspring, the kidnapper had rushed in and tackled Kavoni to the ground like Miles Garrett. Then, with his knees planted on either side of him, he used his hands like hammers and nailed him with a series of bone-breaking blows.

"Feel the pain!" he barked with each blow, though Kavoni had long ago lost consciousness.

Removing his mask, the man placed his nose near Kavoni's face to check for a pulse. Satisfied, he breathlessly rose to his feet and made a brief phone call. "My work here is done."

While Kavoni wouldn't have recognized his assailant, his brother, King, would've. For it was the same man who had spooked him when he and Unique went to visit her cousin in Flint.

Minutes after making the phone call, the man, named Otha, heard the crunching sound of tire on gravel and raised the garage door.

Behind the wheel of a blue minivan was Unique's cousin, Pee-Wee.

Grabbing Kavoni by a wrist and ankle, Otha carried him to the van and slung him inside. Then, after lowering the garage door, he climbed in the back with Kavoni and the van eased out of the alley.

With the sun on the verge of rising as he drove through light traffic, Pee-Wee turned down a back street where he assumed it would be a while before Kavoni's body was discovered.

After pushing the lifeless form out on to asphalt, Otha joined Pee-Wee up front. "The wages of sin," he said, reaching for his seatbelt as the van rolled forward.

Nakedly deserted in the middle of the road, Kavoni was miraculously clinging to life. But with the intake of each painful breath, he could feel his clock winding down. And had he not held his breath when Otha checked to see if he was still breathing, he was certain his time would've already expired.

Fumiya Payne

*Without the strength to move a single muscle, Kavoni was be-
ginning to doubt his ability to survive. The pain he felt was beyond
description. And was it not for his revengeful appetite, he would've
answered death's call.*

*He was on the brink of losing consciousness, when the female
driver nearly ran him over. Unsure if it was the kidnapper returning
or a citizen who just happened to be passing by, Kavoni resumed
playing possum.*

*But when he heard the woman gasp in shock at his condition,
he gathered every ounce of energy left in his body and weakly pled,
"Help me."*

"Oh my God!" she jumped, startled by the fact that he was alive.

*Reaching for her phone, she informed him that she was about
to call an ambulance.*

"No."

*"No?" she repeated in confusion. "Well, what do want me to
do, because you obviously need help?"*

"You... help me. Please."

With the exertion of all his energy, Kavoni passed out.

*Well aware of the crew known throughout the city as "The
N.F.L.", the woman, Tamra, saw an opportunity. Because to help
one of its members would surely earn her some type of monetary
reward. So, she phoned the one person who she knew was capable
of providing the proper care and assistance—her friend, Mecca.*

*"Girl, I need you," Tamra said when Mecca answered. Then,
saying little as possible over the phone, she gave Mecca her location.*

*When Mecca arrived on scene shortly after, she saw Tamra
standing over what appeared to be a dead body.*

*"Bitch, what the fuck is this?" she barked through her partially
lowered window.*

*Hurriedly approaching the car, Tamra explained, "Girl, this
one of them N.F.L. niggas. And I found him on my way to work. He
ain't dead yet, but he will be if he don't get help real soon."*

"Then why call me, and not an ambulance?"

40

"I tried, but he said not to. So, I'm thinking he must be on the run or something. But listen, if you help me, I guarantee it'll work in our favor. And you the only person I know who a real nurse."

Currently an LPN, who was on her way to leveling up a step, Mecca was going to school for her bachelor's degree, while working part-time at a nursing home.

"We can put him your basement," Tamra continued. "And if shit ever hit the fan, which I doubt, I'll take all the blame and say I hid him down there without you knowing."

Nervously glancing over her shoulder for an oncoming car, Tamra took it upon herself to open Mecca's back door. *"Now come help me get him in the backseat."*

"Why we can't put him in your car?"

"Because I ain't got no license. You know that. Now come on."

Exiting her car in reluctance, Mecca went around to the passenger side. *"Bitch, I swear if you get me jammed up..."*

"Grab his legs," Tamra said while grabbing him under the arms.

When she bent down to comply, Mecca gasped in surprise.

Tamra smiled. *"He gotta big dick, don't he?"*

"Nah, I seen him before," she said, eyeing his battered face in recognition. "We was at a Walmart a couple months ago and he fixed my flat tire."

As Mecca recalled their brief encounter, she marveled at the manner in which they'd reunited.

He once helped me, and now it's on me to help him, she thought before grabbing his legs.

***

With his left eye swollen shut and his injured arm in a sling, Kavoni awakened in what appeared to be a small, storage room. Lying on a twin-size air mattress, he attempted to raise up and was seized by sharp pains throughout his entire top half.

As he was groaning in pain, the door to the room opened and he thought he must've died and went to heaven. Because standing *in the doorway was an angel he had been longing to see again, but thought he never would.*

"I gotta be dead," he mumbled to himself, while eyeing her in disbelief.

"Nah, you ain't dead." Mecca smiled. "I don't know how, but you still here."

"So, it's really you?" he said in a raspy voice.

"It really is."

After he was given some water, which he thirstily drank, Kavoni joked, "So this what a nigga had to do to see you again, huh? Damn near get beat to death."

A woman he'd often thought about, Kavoni was not only surprised to see her, but even more amazed by the fact that she was responsible for restoring him back to life. This was a reunion he would've never imagined in a million years.

As the time passed and Mecca assisted in his physical therapy, Kavoni would gradually regain his strength. Before long, he was doing pull-ups from a steel pipe in her basement.

"Well, look at you." Mecca smiled, impressed by the rippling muscles of his arms and back.

Upon completion of his set, Kavoni dropped down from the pipe and used a towel to dry the sweat from his forehead.

"I know I've probably said it a hundred times already." He stared in Mecca's hypnotic green eyes, "But I really do appreciate what you've done for me. And I literally owe you my life. Because without your help, I know I wouldn't have made it."

"For real for real, you need to be thanking my girl, Tamra. Because it was her that found you. I wanted to call an ambulance and get missing."

"But you didn't. And you know why?"

"I just told you."

Kavoni shook his head in disagreement. "Nah, that ain't the reason."

"Then tell me, Mr. Know-It-All."

"I believe the direction of our lives is already mapped out. Now, that ain't saying we can't go off track. But for the most part, we

generally end up where we supposed to. And I knew one day we'd meet again, whether it was here, or in the afterlife. I didn't know it would be under these circumstances, but I believe it was meant for your friend to find me and just so happen to know a nurse named Mecca.''

Kavoni took a step closer and continued. *"This ain't no coincidence. This was by design. I can see it in your eyes that you've been through a lot. And so, have I. So, what better match than two people who can relate to pain and adversity. Mecca, this deeper than what's just on the surface."*

She took a step back to ward off the emotional pull of his words.

"Kavoni, I hear everything you saying, and I'm not disagreeing with you. But right now, we on two different playing fields. I have hopes and dreams that don't involve visiting my man at a prison or a cemetery. And you're right, I have been through a lot. Which would be silly of me to subject myself to what I know will only lead to additional heartache."

Before he could respond, Tamra descended the basement steps. *"What's going on down here?"* she inquired, being nosy, taking in Mecca's flustered expression and Kavoni's muscular frame.

"Ain't shit," Kavoni coolly replied, stretching his neck. *"Just trying to bounce back, you feel me?"*

"Yeah, I see you, player." Tamra smiled. *"Down here flexing for my girl and shit. I just hope when you bounce back, you don't forget who helped you."*

"Tamra!" Mecca exclaimed in a scolding tone.

"Nah, she right," Kavoni said in her defense. *"Because without y'all, I'd probably wouldn't be here. So, it's only right that I pay my medical bill. And soon as I get a chance to move around, I'ma take care of that."*

Later that evening as they were having a quiet dinner, Mecca questioned him in regard to establishing contact with his family. She knew from one of their conversations that he only had a younger brother and a best friend named Puma. *"...You've been here nearly three weeks, and I was just wondering why you haven't reached out yet."*

"To be honest, I really don't know what to think. I mean, clearly, I got kidnapped and damn near killed. So, because I'm assuming they think I'm dead, I'm just trying to figure out how to play it from here."

"You don't think your own peoples were involved, do you?"

"Until I know, I don't know."

"But I'd think you and your brother would be super close, considering it's only the two of y'all."

"Yeah, that's like my son for real. But at the same time, I know that lil' nigga wanted a bigger role. So, I don't know."

"And Puma?"

Kavoni couldn't contain a smile. "That's my heart, right there. I'd hate to find out she had something to do with this. But at this point, I can't put nothing past nobody."

"And let's say you did find out one or both of them was involved. Then what?"

For the sake of Mecca's conscience, Kavoni shrugged. "I can't really say right now. That's a decision I'll have to make when, or if that moment arrives."

"Well, however it happened, at some point you'll have to address it. And from your reaction when I mentioned Puma, I'd start with her."

***

Puma wore a slight frown after listening to Kavoni explain as much of the kidnapping as he could recall. And while she was grateful for his survival, there was something that deeply troubled her and could not be ignored.

"Bro, don't get me wrong, I'm happy as fuck you made it out alive. But you mean to tell me you've been good all this time and you couldn't have called me?"

"I just didn't—"

"Nigga, I was on the verge of killing myself. Do you really understand that?"

When he attempted to reach out and touch her, Puma swatted his hand away and angrily hopped up from the couch. "I seen all that blood in that garage, and I literally threw up my fucking guts. I didn't eat, sleep, or bathe for days. I ain't never felt that much pain in all my life. Even when I was a little girl. And you know what I've been through."

With tears now sliding down her face, Puma continued, "I couldn't even imagine going on without you. I blamed myself for not being there to…" Her words suddenly trailed off as she screwed her face up at Kavoni and asked, "You thought I might've had something to do with it, didn't you?"

A question he'd been hoping she didn't ask, Kavoni shamefully averted his gaze. "Puma, I was so fucked up behind what had happened, I didn't know what to think."

"Answer my question!"

"What would you have thought?'' he countered. "Tell me what you would've honestly thought if roles were reversed."

Before she could answer that he would've been the last person on earth she would've suspected, a soft creak drew their attention to the top of the staircase, where Shawna was standing in a pair of pajamas.

Quickly wiping her face, Puma asked the girl if something was wrong.

Shawna shook her head. "I just heard you talking, that's all."

Kavoni watched their exchange with a puzzled expression. He had never known Puma to have a younger sibling or a close relative.

"Well, there's nothing to worry about," Puma assured her. "I'm good. So go back to bed. You got school tomorrow."

As Shawna complied, Kavoni inquired, "Whose is that?"

"It's a long story."

Rising from the sofa, Kavoni walked over to Puma and pulled her in his arms. "I'm sorry, my baby. And I swear on my mother's grave, I didn't want to think you would do no shit like that. I love you just as much as you love me, if not more. But when you in a position like that, you can't stop your mind from thinking certain shit. But I should've known better than to entertain it. So, for that, I apologize from the bottom of my heart. And I hope you can forgive my weakness."

With her face buried in his chest, Puma slowly nodded in acceptance of his apology. Because like he said, until you're in certain positions, you can only assume how it'll unfold.

As they were back on the sofa, Kavoni listened intently while Puma brought him up to speed with the past month of her life. And when he learned how she came to be in custody of Shawna, he realized it wasn't only he who had been going through something. For Puma had dealt with demons that had been haunting her for a long time. And she done so all alone.

"Damn, girl," Kavoni said, pulling her into his arms. "I hate to hear that you had to go through all of that by yourself. My situation was rough, but I can't even imagine what yours was like."

They were leaning forward in deep thought, when Puma turned to Kavoni and interrupted the silence. "Bro, I already know you've been plotting. So how you plan on handling this situation? Because I'm on whatever you on."

"That's what's up," he said, nodding his head in appreciation. "And you right, I haven't thought about nothing else. And with everything you've told me, I can't help but think that King might be involved. I just need to look that lil' nigga in his eyes. Because either he guilty, or that bitch got him so blind he can't see the scales on her back."

He turned to Puma with a cold stare. "As a child, I promised my mama I'd watch over him as long as I was alive. But if he knowingly played a role in this, then I can't say she'll ever forgive me. Because I'ma make sure they get the chance to meet for the first time."

Chapter 8

At a well-known barber shop on the city's west side, King was seated in the waiting area as Double-O was getting a shape-up. Clad in designer attire and Cartier 'Buffs', it was their newly-obtained chains that gained the most attention. Bright gold and flooded with a fleet of frosted flakes, the Cuban link was accompanied by a large diamond pendant that read, "The F.A.M."

Since scissoring the cord to their former team, King and Double-O decided to emerge under a new umbrella. With less than a dozen men enlisted in their prosperous platoon, their new moniker had been easily and accordingly chosen.

Over bottles of champagne, they'd been in the private booth of a club one night, when King stood up and exclaimed, "It's us against the city! We gon' run this bag up, and whoever don't like can take a dirt nap, you hear me? We might not be deep in number, but we heavy in heart. So, from now on, we known as 'The F.A.M.' Because not only is we family, but we the F.ew A.gainst M.any."

King was exchanging text messages with Unique, when two men marched into the shop, wearing hooded track suits and solemn expressions.

"Aye, let me bark at you outside real quick," Finesse, the shorter of the duo said to King.

He was the owner of the cell phone number Unique had stolen for its clientele. But more interestingly, this was one of Dolphin's leading salesmen.

Amid the attentive eyes of everyone inside the shop, King boldly rose to his feet and replied, "If you came to do something, then get to it. But if not, take that Barry White out your tone, nigga. Fuck wrong with you?"

When the man with Finesse tried to slyly slip a hand under his hoodie, a green beam began flickering over his face, earning his undivided attention.

With his hand hidden beneath the barber cape, Double-O was clutching a full-size Glock.

"I got thirty of these bitches." He smiled, referring to the number of bullets in the gun. "That means I couldn't miss if I wanted to."

Although he wisely replaced his hand back at his side, the man left his demonic eyes locked on to Double-O's.

Masking his inner fear with an amused grin, Finesse returned his attention to King. "Since I'm the one who bought you that chain, then it's only fair I get a chance to wear it." He saluted King before turning to walk out. "See you around."

As they exited the shop, Finesse quietly informed his shooter, "'That nigga dead. So, don't say shit to nobody. We gon' handle this ourself."

Back inside the barber shop, Double-O sent a text to one of his comrades. "Bring me some honeybuns." With the term "honeybun" being the code word for a fifty-round drum, he was simply ensuring that he and King had a president's protection when they made their exit.

Soon after sending the text message, a pair of Dodge Chargers sped up to the barber shop and screeched to a stop.

CJ, the recipient of Double-O's message, emerged from the passenger seat of the lead car and sauntered toward the shop, holding a chrome handgun that was impregnated with a drum full of hollows.

"What's up with the F.A.M.?" he anxiously greeted, unconcerned with the fearful expressions of those inside.

"We good," King cockily assured him, as Double-O was paying for his haircut. "Just some light skin nigga doing a bunch of wolfing!"

In spite of King downplaying the incident, Double-O was actually concerned. The comment in regards to their chains enabled him to quickly make the connection. And just because the man's approach was laughable didn't mean he lacked a crew of killers who'd squeeze on command. And in a game governed by mind and muscle, Double-O knew the victor was usually determined by he who drew first.

As they sped away from the barber shop in a blue Demon, Double-O briefly took his eyes off the road to look at King. "You know that's dog who number we stole, right?"

King nodded, wondering how the theft had been tied back to him.

"Well, we need to bury that nigga soon," Double-O added, "Because you can believe he wanna do the same to us."

They were wordlessly riding out to King's new condo, when he interrupted to silence with a surprising announcement, "I wanna be the one to bury that nigga, bro."

Double-O nodded in acknowledgement, but didn't immediately respond. While he had known this was a conversation that would soon come about, he just hoped King could deal with the aftereffects that came along with killing.

"I ain't even gon' try and talk you out of it," he finally spoke. "But I will say this... once you cross over, ain't no turning back. You either gon' have the stomach for it, or you ain't."

He turned to look King in his eyes. "So, let's see what's you made of, my baby."

***

Three nights later, King and Double-O were parked down the street from the house in which Finesse and his family laid their heads.

With his gloved hand hugging a Glock .23, King had the hood of his track suit tied over his braided locks. He had spoken only a few words since their arrival.

"You nervous as fuck, ain't you?" Double-O grinned.

Despite shaking his head in denial, King's palms were sweating from the reality of how close he was to actually taking someone's life.

"It's alright to be nervous, my baby. Shit, I was on some super nutty shit the first time I put one down."

Adopting a more serious tone, Double-O continued, "But once you run down on this nigga, you gotta fire his ass straight up.

Fumiya Payne

Hesitation get you kilt. So, don't even think about it, just start squeezing. And make sure you get close enough to put at least two in his head."

Minutes later, as Double-O was peering at his side mirror, a cream-colored sedan came sliding down the block. Through the car's light tint, he was able to make out Finesse's face as he drove past.

"Aye...yo, that's him," he alerted King in a hurried tone. "Go do your thang, my baby."

As King skuttled alongside parked cars in a crouched position, his heartbeat was hammering against his chest. Any louder and he knew Finesse would surely hear it.

Time seemed to convert into slow motion as the driver side door of the sedan opened and out stepped Finesse.

Now came the moment of truth.

Forcing himself to react, King rose up and quickly crossed the street, extending his arm in preparation to shoot.

He opened fire just as Finesse was turning around at the feel of someone's presence.

A number of numerous rounds ripped through his upper body, causing him to fall back into the hinge of the car door before slowly sliding downwards.

Recalling Double-O's instructions, King ran closer to finish him off.

As he was standing over a whimpering Finesse, his attention was drawn into the car, where a small child was fearfully watching him from the passenger seat. A drove of tears cascaded over his brown cheeks.

"Please, don't kill my daddy," the nine-year-old pled in a small voice.

With his weapon aimed at Finesse's face, King was uncertain of what to do. To murder a man before the eyes of his child was a boundary he was not sure if he could cross.

But his decision was made when Double-O sped up and yelled through the lowered window, "Bro!"

Snapped out of his trance-like state, King turned to lock eyes with Double-O.

As the two friends maintained eye contact, Double-O said, "Now squeeze."

Without looking at Finesse, King flinchingly fired four rounds into his head. Then, with his heartbeat threatening to burst from inside his chest, he dove inside the car and screamed for Double-O to go.

The Hellcat left its rubber signature on the pavement as it peeled off down the block.

Not until they were a safe distance from the crime scene did Double-O excitedly grab King around the bicep. "Nigga, you good?"

His heart still pumping, he breathlessly nodded, "Yeah, I'm good."

"Nigga, you hit that boy with some shit!" he said in a proud tone. "I knew you had it in you."

Though he flashed a subtle grin, King's mind was consumed by the terrified expression on the little boy's face.

Occasionally glancing at King as they sped down the interstate, Double-O took in his troubled expression and calmly consoled, "It was him or us, my baby. So, you ain't do nothing wrong. And if you want, we can call the troops and go pop champagne."

Declining the offer, King lied and said he had to get home. "I told Unique I wouldn't be out too late, and last thing I need right now is for her to be getting suspicious."

As he pulled up in front King's residence out in Birmingham, Double-O instructed him to trash his track suit and soak his body in a tub of bleach to remove any gunshot residue. "Make sure you do that as soon as you go in. And I'ma get up with you tomorrow, my baby."

While watching King disappear inside the house, Double-O could tell by his demeanor that guilt was already gnawing away at his conscious. He just hoped it wasn't to the point where King would liken Unique to a priest and make an incriminating confession.

Pulling away from the curb, Double-O had one more loose end to tie up before calling it a night. For the man who had accompanied Finesse into the barber shop was to suffer the same fate as his friend's. And Double-O had his address as well.

Chapter 9

"I'm sorry!"

"I'm sorry!"

"I'm sorry!"

Awakened from her sleep by King's repetitive screams, Unique grabbed ahold of his arm and shook him. "King!"

His trembling body covered in sweat, his eyes popped open, filled with a reflection of genuine terror.

"Baby, what's wrong?"

For a moment he just stared at her as if seeing a ghost, then hopped up and ran to the bathroom.

Seconds later, Unique could hear him throwing up. In all the time they'd been together, she had never known him to have nightmares. So, she knew it was caused by something that had recently happened. And she was certain it was associated with the strange behavior he exhibited upon his return home the night before.

As he hovered over the toilet, Unique leaned against the bathroom's doorway and crossed her arms. "You want to tell me what's going on?"

Slowly shaking his head, he looked over his shoulder with reddened eyes, "He won't go away."

"Who?"

His eyes took on a faraway expression before he whispered, "The little boy."

In his dream, King had been in an unfamiliar neighborhood, when he spotted the little boy coming toward him. Immediately turning to head in the opposite direction, he glanced over his shoulder and saw the boy was following him. King took off running. And though he was pumping his legs harder than Usain Bolt, he was moving in slow motion. Unable to lose the boy, he ducked off inside an abandoned building. And much to his dismay, the boy came inside shortly after.

"What do you want?" King had breathlessly demanded.

The little boy walked within several feet and carefully reached in his pocket to remove something.

King stared in horror at the boy's hand.

Inside his small palm was a human heart... that no longer pulsed.

King fearfully jumped back when he tossed the heart near his feet.

With tears streaming from his innocent eyes, the little boy softly asked, "Why you kill my daddy?"

Not knowing what to say, King could only shake his head and apologize, "I'm sorry."

"But he was my only daddy. And he loved me. Why would you take him?"

"I'm so sorry," King repeated, his own eyes beginning to tear up.

The boy's face suddenly took on a demonic appearance and he lunged at King, gripping him with the strength of an adult. "Why you kill my daddy?"

"I'm sorry! I'm sorry! I'm sorry!"

At the recollection of his nightmare, King involuntarily shivered.

"Come on, daddy, let's get you in the shower," Unique said, helping him to his feet.

After cleaning the floor and toilet, she joined him under the steaming water. Removing the washcloth from his hand, she began to gently bathe him before urging, "Now tell mama what happened."

Beginning with the barber shop incident, he described every detail of yesterday's events. Then, as he gave a tearful account of the actual killing, Unique cradled him against her bosom and comforted him in a motherly tone, "It's ok, love. You made a mistake. But from now on, I need you to focus on just being King, and let your pawns play their position."

She tilted his head to where she could look in his eyes. "My love for you is unconditional. At this point, I'm all in. So, I don't want you out here doing extra shit that can take you away from me. I need you. Can you understand that, King?"

When he nodded, she trailed kisses from his lips to his lower half.

"This my best friend." She smiled before savoring the head like a chocolate lollipop. "And I don't know what I'd do without him. So, you better not make me find out."

As she gazed upwards with a dreamy expression, Unique proceeded to give him her famous "turtle's neck," otherwise known as "slow head."

Closing his eyes with a pleasurable groan, King surrendered to the skills of her scholarly mouth. Because she clearly had a degree in headology.

With her nails clutching his thighs, she lovingly rotated her head in various directions, while her restless tongue slithered over his enlarged veins.

"I love him," she tried to say without removing it from her mouth.

"I couldn't hear you." He smiled.

When she repeated it, then forced him down her throat and began loudly gagging, he grabbed a fistful of her hair and came with the cry of a wounded animal.

As they were lying in bed later that morning, watching the movie *Queen and Slim*, Unique suddenly lifted her head up from King's chest and inquired, "Daddy, you didn't bring that gun in here, did you?"

At the sight of his guilty expression, she scolded him, "King, how could you be so reckless? Don't you know that's a life sentence?"

"I'ma get rid of it. I just wanted to come home first. But soon as -"

She shook her head, "That thing gotta get up out of here right now. I ain't trying to spook you, but that little boy could identify you. And the worst thing you want to do is to get caught with the murder weapon."

"I'm saying, but I don't know where—"

She firmly grabbed his face in her hands, "Listen carefully. I'ma take care of it this one time, but don't ever put me in no position like this again. Because what good am I to you if I'm locked up?"

Grateful and relieved to have a woman as gritty as Unique, he willingly informed her of the gun's location.

"Alright, I'll be right back," she said, kissing his cheek before leaving the room.

Retrieving the murder weapon from inside the living room couch, Unique wore a subtle grin as she placed it in her purse. Because unbeknownst to King, her motive for volunteering to dispose of the gun was beyond anything he could've ever imagined.

King was anxiously awaiting her return, when he was startled by the sound of his doorbell. Upon checking the screen of his iPad, which showed the condo's parameter, he noticed a lone figure standing at the front door.

"Damn!" he cursed to himself.

Moments later came a series of loud knocks.

Exiting the bed with a loud sigh, King headed downstairs to unlock the front door.

"Fuck you got your phone turned off for?" Double-O said he walked in. "And why the fuck is you looking like your dog just died?"

"That shit fucking with me, bro," King admitted. "Like, on some heavy shit. I even dreamed about it."

Double-O nodded, as if that was what he had expected. Then he had a sudden thought that caused his eyebrows to crease into a curious frown. "Aye, bro, where that gun at?"

King looked away and lied, "I already got rid of it."

Studying his best friend for a trace of dishonesty, he decided King was being untruthful. Not out of deceit, but fear of displeasing him.

"I rock with you from the heart, bro," Double said. "So, you ain't never gotta lie to me about me nothing. You already know I ain't gon' look down on you or judge you. But I will try to fix whatever mistakes you make. So just be sure to keep that in mind."

King nodded but refrained from revealing the truth about what he'd done with the gun.

Deciding he would revisit the subject at a later date, Double-O instead addressed the state of distress under which King was buried.

"I need you to listen to me," he said in a tone that drew King's eye contact. "I know that shit eating at you. And if you keep sitting up here like this, you gon' fuck around and lose your marbles, my nigga. So, the only thing you can do now is deaden your conscience."

"How?" King quickly inquired. At this point he'd do almost anything to erase the image of the little boy.

"You gon' have to do another one."

King looked at Double-O as if he had lost his mind.

"I'm serious, bro," he persisted. "It gets easier as you do 'em. I told you ain't no coming back once you cross over. So, either lose your fucking mind, or suit and get busy."

After taking a long moment to ponder over Double-O's advice, King turned to head upstairs.

"What up?" Double-O called out.

King answered without looking back, "I'm about to go get dressed."

Fumiya Payne

Chapter 10

"Marriage... got it out the mud, it was ugly/ Average... I can't go back to having nothing/ Savage... product of my environment, I'm hustling/ Carats... clarity gon' glisten when it's dirty."

Gripping the wheel in one hand a Ruger in the other, Kavoni was vibing to Future's song, "The Way Things Going" as he drove down the interstate in a white H3 Hummer. En route to the dealership in Dearborn, he was hoping to reinstate his arrangement with the Mexicans.

Driven insane by his conflicted emotions, Kavoni had hardly slept over the past few days. Though King's betrayal would be deserving of death, he was saddened by the thought of slaying his own sibling. But in their world, where rules were essentially nonexistent, he knew the softhearted were usually devoured. To prevail amongst piranhas, one had to become an extreme product of his environment. It was eat or be eaten.

Pulling into the dealership, Kavoni parked near the front entrance and killed the music.

When the usual female employee emerged from the building minutes later, he reached in the backseat to retrieve a black duffel bag.

"May I help you?" she asked, displaying no visible signs of recognition. She was eyeing him as he if they'd never met.

Irritated by her behavior, Kavoni replied, "Yeah, can you tell Mr. Morales that Kavoni McClain out here."

"I'm sorry, sir, but there's no one here by that name."

He smirked, recalling what Puma had said in regards to her unsuccessful trip. Glancing at the bag full of money, which he owed from the shipment prior to the kidnapping, he knew his water supply had officially been cut off.

Before throwing the H3 in drive, he left the woman with a parting message for the Mexicans. "You tell them Kavoni McClain said he'd fuck a monkey in the ass before he ever dropped a dime on anybody!"

On account of his sudden and prolonged disappearance, he knew they were thinking at some point he had gotten jammed up. And due to the quantity and quality of the drugs, to reappear surely meant he had cooperated in exchange for a lighter sentence. While he couldn't necessarily blame them for being suspicious, he was still angered by the thought of his character being questioned. Especially when it pertained to snitching.

As he was exiting the dealership, Kavoni slammed on the brakes. Then, making a decision that most would've considered crazy, he grabbed the duffel bag and tossed it out the window.

"I'ma always be a man of my word," he vowed while driving off, leaving behind five hundred grand.

While heading back to Detroit, Kavoni was pondering over the plummet of his once prosperous life. The rapidness in which everything crumbled was mind blowing. And though he despised Unique with a passion, he had no choice but to salute her savagery. Because without lifting a finger, she managed to dismantle his entire operation. But he knew there was one thing she hadn't been banking on, his survival.

His fantasy of slowly filleting Unique before removing her head was interrupted by the vibration of his phone.

"What up, doe?" he greeted.

"Oh, so that's how you answer your phone?" Mecca teased on the other end. "All hood and stuff?"

"I'm saying, I can get on some professional shit," he smiled. "But I didn't know I had to carry it with you like that. With your saddity ass."

"No, you didn't!" she laughed. "But since I'm so saddity, then tell me why my car done broke down and I'm sitting in the middle of traffic, looking silly."

Kavoni's foot unconsciously bore down on the gas pedal. "Where you at?"

Upon hearing the location, he assured her he'd be there shortly. "I'm right outside the city. Just give me like ten, fifteen minutes."

When he arrived on scene, Kavoni parked behind her battered Honda and hit his hazard lights.

Salute my Savagery 2

As they simultaneously exited their cars, Kavoni shook his head in amusement.

"What?" Mecca smiled, looking super cute in her pink scrubs and Hello Kitty Crocs.

"Nah, it's just that this car stay giving you problems."

"I know, right?" She laughed. "But it's hard out here for a pimp. So, I gotta make do for right now."

"It might be time for the pimp to get an upgrade," he said, lifting the hood of her car. "Because you too damn pretty to be out here stranded on side of the road."

After pretending to perform a thorough inspection, he slammed the hood and delivered the bad news. "Welp, it look like this mu'fucka ready to go to the scrap yard. But the good thing is, they'll probably give you a few hundred for it."

"What's wrong with it?" she genuinely inquired.

"A whole bunch of shit."

Mecca squinted her eyes at him in skepticism. "You don't know what the hell you doing, do you?"

"Hell nah!" he started laughing. "But I do know it's time to cop something else. This thing on its last leg."

"Yeah, well, until I get this degree and go up to RN, I gotta work with what I got, player. And I just need to be able to get back and forth to work, anyway."

After calling a tow truck, Kavoni and Mecca climbed in the Hummer to wait for its arrival.

"What you over there thinking about?" she asked upon noticing his thoughtful expression.

"You," he truthfully answered.

When she didn't respond, he turned to her and continued, "Mecca, I ain't even gon' lie, I've been thinking about you since the first time we met. I used to see people with their girls, and it would make me think about what it would be like if you were mines. And I told myself when we crossed paths again, I'd do whatever it took to find out. I ain't never had feelings like this for no other woman. So, I just need you to tell me what I gotta do to be a part of your life."

"Kavoni, I think you're a very handsome man. And I don't doubt that you probably gotta good heart. But I just can't get involved with a street dude. I've been losing loved ones all my life to the streets. So, I'm fully aware of what would come with dealing with you. And, boo, I'm sorry, but I already got enough heartache to last me a lifetime."

Kavoni slowly shook his head in disappointment. It seemed like things you wanted most were always the things you couldn't have.

"I'm not trying to hurt your feelings, or make you feel a sense of rejection," Mecca added. "But I gotta do what's best for my heart. And I would hope you could understand."

"I hear you, Mecca. But you acting like a nigga plan on being in the game forever."

"Kavoni, it only takes a split second to end up in a cell or a cemetery. You know that."

"I come from the mud, sweetheart, and that's my reality. If I knew a safer route to the bag, I'd take it without hesitation. But I don't. So, for right now, it's stack or starve. I just can't believe you willing to go against something that's clearly meant to be. They say all great accomplishments are hard earned. That means you gotta put in work for what you want, whether it's a relationship or a career."

He sensed from her expression that his words were having an effect and continued, "I can see it in them pretty ass eyes, you've been through a lot. So, the last thing I wanna do hurt you. But sometimes life will give us a blessing that might not come in the form we imagined. So, we gotta be able to use our own wisdom and discernment to recognize certain things and people for what and who they are. It's said when you meet your other half, you'll know it. And I know you feel the connection and chemistry between us. So, see this for what it is, Mecca. And just give me one year, and I promise I'll cut all ties to the streets."

Taking a deep breath and slowly exhaling, she was on the verge of responding, when she was saved by the arrival of the tow truck.

Grateful for the timely intrusion, she patted Kavoni's thigh before hopping out the Hummer. "We'll revisit this conversation later."

62

Watching her through the front windshield, Kavoni could only wonder what kind of experience caused Mecca to place her heart in a cast.

After her car was loaded onto the flatbed, she returned to inform Kavoni that she'd be accompanying the driver back to the shop. "He said it's something minor, and should be fixed in a couple hours. But I'll definitely be reaching out later so we can continue that conversation. And I got some choice words for you, Mr. McClain."

As Kavoni merged back into traffic, he replaced his thoughts of Mecca, for those of King. It was time for him and the little one to link up. And no matter the verdict, in this instance Kavoni would be the judge, jury and executioner.

Fumiya Payne

Chapter 11

Kavoni and Puma were parked in the vacant field beside their house on Joann Street. He specifically chose this location so he could gauge King's reaction at being in close proximity of the garage. If he had involvement of any kind with his kidnapping, then Kavoni was certain his trained eye would recognize even the slightest sign of guilt.

With his insulated trunk housing what sounded to be a marching band, King's arrival was preceded by the deep bass of his stereo system.

As he came flying up the block in his candy-painted Cutlass, King was being trailed by a money-green Chevelle that belonged in a car show. Screeching to a loud stop, the thirty-inch wheels of both cars enabled them to easily climb up onto the curb.

King swung the Cutlass around so that its gold grille was facing the street. Then, once the Chevelle followed suit, he and Double-O exited the car and left their doors open, for they had no intentions of a long stay.

Because it was Puma who had summoned the meeting, both men were surprised to see Kavoni emerge from the passenger seat of the Hellcat, proudly wearing his N.F.L. chain.

"What's good lil' bro?" Kavoni smiled. "You look like you seen a ghost."

Quickly regrouping, King shot back, "Shit, that's what it feel like, the way your ass just up and disappeared."

Playing the background, Double-O cut his eyes at Puma in distaste. For she had summoned their presence under the false pretenses of a business proposal.

As the two siblings were holding one another's stare, Kavoni was able to notice something that was slightly startling. *This lil' nigga done put in some work*, he correctly concluded to himself. When a man has killed on more than one occasion, there was a look in his eyes only another killer could see.

Fumiya Payne

Checking the time on his plain-faced Rolex, King impatiently inquired, "So, what's on your mind, my baby? Because clearly y'all didn't call me here for a staring match."

"So, that's the vibe now, huh?" Kavoni smirked. "You seeing a few dollars and now you've forgotten everything else."

King looked away and sucked his teeth.

"What happened to Never Forsake Love or Loyalty?" Kavoni implored as he took in his brother's new chain. "How you let some pussy come between your own blood?"

"Ain't nothing came between nothing. Nigga, I damn near begged you to put me in the game, but you kept ignoring me. So, you can't be mad an opportunity presented itself and I took it."

"You in over your head, King. I wasn't ignoring you; I was protecting you. Because no matter how hard you try, I didn't raise you to be a drug dealer. You letting that bitch call all the shots. I know what's going on, my baby."

King looked at Double-O and scoffed, "You hear this nigga, bro? He clearly don't know what the fuck going on out here."

Turning back to Kavoni, King lifted his chin and boasted, "Not only am I feeding my whole team, but nigga, we out here boxing shit, you hear me? So put some respect on that shit. Because it ain't about what you raised, it's about who I became!"

Kavoni lost control of his emotions at King's false sense of bravado.

"I done buried many niggas!" he snarled through gritted teeth, taking a step closer. "And I sleep like a baby at night. Can you say the same, muthafucka? Huh?"

The expression in King's eyes enabled Kavoni to know that he had struck a nerve.

Seething from the accuracy of his brother's assumption, he turned to Double-O. "Come on, bro, we out. I done heard enough of this shit."

On instinct, Kavoni glanced towards the Chevelle, where a pair of eyes were watching him with the intensity of a hawk.

As the two cars rolled off the curb, CJ came out the sunroof of the Chevelle and turned to face Kavoni. Clutching a fully auto

66

Glock, he emptied the clip into the clouds as they sped off down the block.

This your warning, CJ was basically stating.

After watching the cars bend the corner and disappear out of sight, Puma interrupted Kavoni's thoughts with an inquiry, "So, what's the verdict?"

Shaking his head, he answered, "He ain't gotta clue. And I ain't just saying that because he my brother, that's really how I feel."

Aside from paying no attention to the garage, King displayed no noticeable signs of deception. He may have been guilty of being stubborn and misled, but he was innocent of all else.

"But that bitch, Unique," Kavoni shook his finger accusingly, "We gon' have to run a fifty on her. Because we already know she a snake. But now I wanna know what hole she slithered out of."

Puma nodded in agreement. "Yeah, I'ma have to have a serious talk with Jazz. Because she the one brought her around. So, she definitely got some explaining to do."

As they were riding through traffic, entertaining their own thoughts, a bulb of enlightenment suddenly went off in Kavoni's head. He spotted a nearby Auto Zone and told Puma to pull into it. "I wanna see if this one girl still work there right quick."

When she parked near the front entrance, Kavoni asked if she would accompany inside.

Not until they were inside the semi-crowded store did Kavoni reveal his true intentions. "I think I figured it out."

"Figured what out?" Puma anxiously inquired.

"The kidnapping, the burglary, all of it."

Kavoni approached a middle-aged male employee and asked if the manager was around.

"You're looking at him." The man smiled.

"Is there somewhere we can speak in private?"

Based on Kavoni's vibe and well-groomed appearance, the manager decided he posed no threat and led them to a small office.

"So, how can I help you?" he asked from a neatly arranged desk.

Before uttering another word, Kavoni removed a bankroll from his pocket and peeled off a thousand dollars.

"I'ma be straight up with you," he said, laying the money on the desk. "I think somebody tracking my car, and I need you to check it out."

As both the manager and Puma raised their eyebrows, Kavoni quickly inserted for the man's benefit, "It ain't law enforcement. It's my ex-wife. We going through a custody battle and she'll use any dirt she can to take my kid."

With the wheels of greed internally turning, the manager briefly eyed the money before looking back up at Kavoni. "I mean, I don't know, man. I could lose my job behind something like this."

Reading in between the lines, Kavoni peeled off another grand.

After scooping up the money quicker than a player would a fumbled football, the manager followed them outside to the Hellcat.

"I'll jack her up and see what I find," he said, accepting the keys from Puma. "Shouldn't take no more than a few minutes."

As they waited, Puma asked Kavoni what made him think of a tracker being on the car.

"Just a hunch," he shrugged.

The manager brought the car back ten minutes later and stepped out with a blank expression.

He slipped a small object into Kavoni's hand and whispered, "That was under the car, by the trunk area. Someone's definitely been tracking your every move."

"It was the only one?"

He nodded. "Now, if you'll excuse me, I need to get back to work."

Closing his hand over the small tracker, Kavoni smirked, "So this how they knew our every move. Probably had one on my car, too. That's how they caught me slipping."

Suggesting they grab lunch at a nearby restaurant, Kavoni scanned their surroundings along the way. Because for all he knew, someone could be stalking them at that very moment.

After quietly establishing their next best move over burgers and fries, Kavoni accidentally bumped into an older white man as they were leaving out. "Excuse me, sir," he apologized while smoothly slipping the tracker in the man's coat pocket.

As they reluctantly returned to the Hellcat and climbed in, Puma said the purple was no longer popping. "It's time to switch the color up, you feel me?"

"What you got in mind?"

A question to which she already had an answer, she smiled. "You'll see."

Fumiya Payne

Chapter 12

Returning home from work at nearly 3 a.m., Jazz tiredly entered her darkened house. She flicked a light switch and shrieked at the surprising sight of Puma, who was planted in the center of her sofa.

With her hand hugging Martha as she wore a cold expression, Puma was seated beside an open suitcase, where a stack of money laid on top of folded clothing.

"What's going on, Puma?" Jazz nervously inquired, as her attention was torn between the gun and suitcase.

"Shit, you tell me," Puma replied, rising to her feet. "Because it seem you the one who planning on taking a trip somewhere."

Jazz frowned in alleged confusion. "And why would I be doing that?"

Growing impatient with the reindeer games, Puma said, "So you really gon' stand there and act like I ain't find this suitcase in your closet?"

"Hell yeah, I am. Especially when it's something I don't know nothing about."

"It's twenty-five racks in this muthafucka!" Puma said, picking up the stack of money. "But you don't know nothing about it."

She tossed the money aside and grabbed different articles of clothing. "This is shit I've personally seen you wearing before, but you don't know nothing about it."

Eyeing the items with a perplexed expression, Jazz shook her head in denial, "Puma, I'm telling you, I don't know how that shit got in there. Yeah, the clothes and suitcase are mine, but the money ain't. And I can't tell you where it came from because I didn't put in there.''

As Puma glared at Jazz, she was thinking about the ransom money, wondering if those were a portion of the same bills. Because in spite of Jazz earning a decent living from dancing, her monthly expenses would've made it impossible for her to save up twenty-five grand. So, unless there was another believable explanation for the money's origin, then she was certain that was a quarter of the ransom she'd paid to Kavoni's kidnappers.

Fumiya Payne

"So, I guess you don't know nothing about the bitch Unique, either, huh?" Puma asked, abruptly changing directions.

"I mean… besides meeting her at the club, nah, not really. And she don't even work there no more, so I really ain't been seeing her now. But she was more cooler with the bartender, May-May, anyway.''

Puma cocked her gun back and caused a shell casing to spit out the side. That was her way of proving that the gun was fully loaded.

"I don't think you hearing me," she said, closing the distance between them in a threatening manner. "Because if you can't tell me about a bitch you introduced into my circle, then that means y'all must be in cahoots."

"Girl, if you really think I was involved with that shit, then you need to seriously consider getting some help. Because you clearly done lost your fucking mind. As I've stated on multiple occasions, I've been down for you since day-muthafucking-one. So, for you to have the audacity to question my character like this is wild as fuck to me. I'm the ally, not the enemy."

Ignoring the gun, Jazz walked closer and placed her hands on either side of Puma's face. "I don't know what I gotta do to prove that my love is real. But I ain't giving up on you, girl. I know you've been through some shit, and I wish you would tell me about it so I can understand you better. But I'll wait until you're ready."

"And as God is my witness," Jazz continued, "I'm looking you in your eyes right now and telling you I would never betray you. I know what Kavoni meant to you. So, there's no way I could've took part in something like that. Or even had any knowledge of it. In hindsight, I can say I shouldn't have never brought old girl around. But I didn't think giving her a ride would lead to all this. But if you're really convinced she did it, then you give me the gun and I'll put her down myself."

Taking a deep breath, Puma retreated several steps and placed her hands on top of her head in a state of confliction.

Jazz grabbed Puma by her hoodie and reigned her back in. "Tell me you've missed me,'' she whispered against Puma's slightly parted lips. "Then tell me what I gotta do to prove I would never

72

cross you. I'm willing to do whatever to earn your trust. That's how much I love and care for you."

Before Puma could answer, Jazz kissed her with enough passion to evoke a sensuous moan from her.

As Puma returned the kiss with the same level of intensity, Jazz reached down to gently remove the gun from her hand. Laying it aside, she enclosed her arms around Puma and surrendered to the pleasurable feel of their entwining tongues.

"Let's go upstairs," Jazz huskily breathed into Puma's mouth. "I need to feel you inside me."

Once they were in her bedroom, Jazz removed a strap-on named Louie from her dresser. Long as a baby's arm but thick as an adult's wrist, the beige accessory resembled a baseball bat, hence its nickname.

"Punish this pussy!" Jazz pled as Puma strapped up and mounted her in missionary position.

Eager to oblige, Puma placed Jazz's legs over her shoulders and reached down to insert Louie.

"Oooh!" Jazz deeply moaned as the sizeable head slid past the swollen lips of her yoni.

With Puma working her hips with the expertise of a porn star, Jazz was soon behaving in a delirious manner. She cried, clawed, cursed, and called out to a God to whom she rarely prayed.

Screaming at a volume that would surely rupture her vocal cords, she praised Puma for a performance that was worthy of being recorded.

As Jazz was on the brink of an orgasm, Puma suddenly pulled out and ordered for her to turn over.

While trembling from the effects of great sex, Jazz readily complied. It had felt like an eternity since their last moment of intimacy, and she was now being reminded of just how explosive the encounters were.

With her face buried in the pillow and spine deeply arched, Jazz released the wail of a newborn as Puma forcefully reentered her.

"Nah, don't run!" she barked, filling her womb in reckless abandonment. "This what you wanted, remember?"

Familiar with the route to Jazz's spot, Puma grabbed her by the hair and began targeting her lower left wall.

Hollering as if she was going into labor, Jazz's quivering thighs and vaginal contractions were signs of an oncoming orgasm. "Harder! Harder!" she demanded, as she was just moments away from a weightless enrapture.

When Jazz screamed in release, Puma jerked her head back, then spit a razorblade out of her mouth and reached around to cut Jazz's throat from ear-to-ear. As blood squirted clear across the room, she continued to sex Jazz in a merciless fashion.

Despite the sincerity in which Jazz had uttered her innocence, her death had already been decreed in Puma's mind. She had brought a snake into her circle. And whether it was intentional or not, it was an error that could neither be excused or overlooked. But on the strength of their history, she'd sent her off with a bang.

After pouring a trail of gasoline from the bedroom to the front door downstairs, Puma struck a match and tossed it. As the flames began slithering its way along the trail, she pulled her hood over her head and unhurriedly exited the burning house.

Chapter 13

Wearing somber expressions as they stepped out of a dark-colored coupe, Dolphin and Nooni walked toward the front door of a two-story townhouse. They were paying a visit neither man looked forward to but knew was necessary.

Seconds after knocking, the door was opened by a petite young woman with bags beneath her red-brimmed eyes. Still in deep mourning over the loss of her first love, she was the mother of Finesse's child.

"Come in," she softly invited, stepping aside for them to enter.

Impressed by the interior layout, Dolphin was proud of his slain soldier, for he could tell he had taken considerable pride in providing for his home front.

The widow offered refreshments, which both men politely declined.

After expressing his condolences in person, Dolphin got to the heart of the matter. "Keisha, I know it's a rough time for you right now, and I could never fully understand your pain. But Finesse was my lil' mans, and it's my duty to make sure his death don't go unpunished. Ain't nothing I can do to bring him back, but loyalty won't allow me to just look the other way."

Wiping a tear from her eye as she slowly nodded, Keisha turned to leave the room.

She returned a minute later, holding the hand of the little boy who had witnessed his father's murder.

Dolphin knelt down so that he and the boy were eye level. "How you feeling, lil' man?"

"I'm ok," he quietly answered.

"You the man of the house now. So, you gotta be strong for your mama, you hear me?"

He nodded.

"Me and your father was good friends," Dolphin continued, "and he didn't deserve what happened to him. So, I need you to do something for me that would really make him proud of you. Can you do that?"

At the mention of pleasing his father, the little boy nodded with more enthusiasm.

"I need you to think back to the night and tell me exactly what you remember."

Because of the boy's age, authorities had sought the mother's permission to interview him. They explained that though it would be a painful recollection, her son could possibly point out the person or people responsible for this senseless crime. However, upon gaining her approval, the interview went nowhere, as the little boy said he never saw the assailant's face. His father had schooled him on the importance of never talking to the police, and he'd honor his counsel until he joined him in heaven.

"I remember everything," the little boy confessed. "But I didn't tell twelve."

Dolphin smiled. "And you did right. But now I need you to tell Uncle Dolph what you saw."

Staring at his hands, which he fidgeted with, he began to explain how him and his father had returned from his little league football game. "We was about to go back out and get some pizza and stuff, and he told me to wait in the car. Then when he got out, that's when he got shot and fell. Then some man came up and saw me in the car."

He paused as tears started to slide down his face and Dolphin gently probed, "Then what happened after that?"

He answered barely above a whisper, "I asked him not to kill my daddy."

This being her first time hearing the horrific account, Keisha rushed over to embrace her son. "Oh my God, baby, I'm so sorry you had to go through something like that. And you should've told me."

Dolphin and Nooni exchanged a brief look, both disturbed by the child's experience. Which made finding out who did it all the more important.

"Lil' man, I got one more question I need to ask you, ok?"

His eyes cast downwards, he slowly nodded.

"What did that bad man look like?"

76

He looked up and pointed at Nooni. "He was his color. And he had a real big tattoo on his neck."

"Did you see what the tattoo was?"

He shook his head.

"What about his hair?"

"He had on a hood."

Dolphin thanked the little boy for his help and said his father would be proud of him.

"Baby, I need you to go back to your room, ok?" Keisha said to her son. "And I'll be up there in a minute."

He turned to leave, then paused at the bottom of the staircase and looked back at Dolphin. "Are you gon' kill that bad man?"

Looking at the mother, then back at the little boy, Dolphin properly replied, "I'ma shoot him twice as many times as he shot your daddy."

The boy flashed a pleased smile before racing upstairs.

"Do you think telling him that was a good idea?" Keisha asked.

"That lil' nigga did something a lot of these grown-ass niggas can't do," Dolphin reasoned. "Which is keeping their mouths shut. So, if that lil' nigga could do that, then he damn sure need to know we gon' avenge the death of his daddy."

Removing a loaf of money from inside his jacket, Dolphin held it out to Keisha. "Until we figure this shit out, I think you should change locations for a minute. And I know it's gon' be a lot of painful memories in this house, so if you want to make the change permanent, just let me know and I'll cover the expenses."

"Thank you so much," Keisha said in gratitude before giving both men a hug. "And just so y'all know, the funeral next Tuesday."

Assuring her they'd be in attendance, Dolphin and Nooni exited the house.

"We gotta find this nigga," Dolphin declared as Nooni awakened the engine. "Because ain't no way Finesse people should be the only ones going to a funeral next week."

Before pulling off, Nooni looked at Dolphin. "I know this might sound crazy, but when that lil' nigga said dog had a big-ass tattoo on his neck, a certain face instantly popped into my head."

"Who?"

"That nigga, King, bro. You know him and Kavoni got them big-ass N.F.L. logos tattooed on their shit."

"Nah, I don't know," Dolphin lightly chuckled. "Because that nigga ain't no killer. Now maybe if you had said Double-O, or somebody, then I could've seen that. But, King... I don't see him the having the heart to stand up over a nigga like that.''

"But on the strength of your intuition," Dolphin added, "We gon' look into it. I've been wrong on a number of occasions. But I do hope I'm right this time, because boxing that nigga would definitely be a conflict of interest."

Referring to the history and business between himself and Puma, Dolphin could only imagine how things would unfold if they had to kill King.

As they drove through traffic, Dolphin got on social media to see if he could find a picture of King. Because if the little boy identified him as being the shooter, then there would certainly be another funeral next week.

Chapter 14

In the crowded parking lot of a Coney Island restaurant, Unique and her friend, May-May, were comfortably settled in a late model Range Rover. Their appearances immaculate, both women's eyes were obscured behind over-sized Chanel shades.

"Look at these hot-ass niggas," Unique softly fumed, as she took in King and his crew. "They just begging for federal indictments."

In Hellcats, Demons, and Durango's, King and his team were racing up and down the street like it was legal. One car in particular had hooligans hanging out the windows and sunroof as it did donuts in the middle of the street. Then, emerging from among a cloud of smoke, it screamed off down the block, with its backend fishtailing.

Undoubtedly in need of new tires, the four vehicles recklessly sped into the Coney Island and skidded to a stop.

Leaving the car doors open as they hopped out, one of the men went live on *Instagram*. "It's the Few Against Many, you feel me! We out here treating Hellcats like Hondas!"

He then focused the camera on a shirtless King, whose Amiri pockets were stuffed with loaves of money.

"...White Buffs no ice, these plain. Posted in the hood wit' all ten of my chains..."

Rapping along with 42-Dugg as he blared from one of the cars, King was proudly displaying his latest purchase, an icy medallion that read, "King Fetty."

Two others appeared beside him, brandishing black handguns equipped with green beams and fifty-round drums.

Planted in the background was Double-O, who was observing the spectacle with a subtle smirk. Though he personally preferred to play it discreetly, he understood the reasons behind their behavior. Just watch the excitement of a starving dog that's suddenly fed.

"I can't stomach no more of this shit," Unique disgustedly uttered while reaching for her phone.

When King answered, she summoned his presence in a stern tone.

As King and May-May traded places in the passenger seat, she headed in Double-O's direction. Unique had convinced her to cut back into him, but with a softer approach.

No sooner than King shut the door did Unique ask him, "So what, you'd rather sleep in a twin-size bed than the one we got at home?"

He frowned in confusion. "What you mean by that?"

"Nigga, what kind of beds you think they got in the feds?"

"We was just having some fun."

"King, you can't afford to have fun right now. When you start getting real money, you gotta fall back from the spotlight. Because you ain't just gotta worry about being seen by the law, but also these heartless, hungry-ass niggas that'll kill you for your glasses alone. And they ain't gon' do you the favor of putting you in a cage, they gon' put your ass in a grave!"

As he wore a receptive expression, she continued, "You not the servant no more, daddy. So, unless you want to give your position up, then I suggest you put a leash on that shit. Because, nigga, you fooling. You all on social media with a chain that say King Fetty. If you was to get indicted, you wouldn't have to worry about nobody telling on you. Because you doing that your damn self." Unique laid a hand on his forearm. "Am I making sense to you, daddy?"

His head down, he slowly bobbed it.

"Alright, well let's stick to the script and keep running this bag up. Then once we relocate to another city and open up some businesses and shit, then you can let your hair down a lil' bit. But until then, I'ma need you to keep in mind which bed you'd rather be sleeping in. Now come over and give mama some sugar."

After sharing a slow, sensuous kiss, Unique said, "I'm your number one fan, daddy. And all I want to do is see you win. I told you in the beginning I'd hold you down, and that's exactly what the fuck I've been doing. Just look at how far you've came since we've been together. Now, if that ain't proof that you fucking with the livest bitch in the city, then I don't know what to tell you."

Meanwhile, Double-O and May-May were quietly conversing as they leaned against the back of a red Durango. She had apologized for her past behavior and recommended they start over. Nonchalant as usual, he had given his consent with a subtle nod.

"You a lot different than these other niggas out here," she truthfully commented. "They be on some wild, obnoxious shit. But you just be chilling, peeping everything." May-May turned to look up at him and smiled, "I like that about you."

Double-O smirked. "Is that right?"

Whether her intentions were innocent or not, Double-O had no interest in even forming a friendship with May-May. In fact, she had a better chance at gaining access inside the Pentagon than she did in his heart. But for the sake of maintaining the peace, until he could put her down without arousing suspicion, he'd adopt a more cordial attitude.

In the midst of May-May joking with Double-O, his comrade, CJ, walked over and rudely cut in, "Aye, bro, remember that Finesse nigga that got kilt last week?"

Maintaining a poker face, though his heartbeat took off running, Double-O casually nodded.

"Man, I just heard that was one of Dolphin's lil' men," CJ informed him. "And they say they boxed that nigga right in front of his nine-year-old son."

As CJ went on rambling, Double-O had tuned him out. Furious at both King and Unique, he cut his eyes toward the Range Rover. He wondered how King had failed to mention anything about the son's presence. And more interestingly, he wondered if Unique was aware of the connection between Dolphin and Finesse when she'd stolen that number.

That bitch might be more vicious than I thought, Double-O considered to himself. Which suddenly explained May-May's persistence. If they could control the narrative on both ends, then they'd surely succeed in whatever scheme they had devised.

Telling May-May it was a pleasure to chat but he had business to attend, Double-O excused himself and summoned King with a wave of the hand.

Once they were alone inside the Durango, he questioned King in regard to Finesse's son being present at the time of the murder.

81

"Where you hear that at?"

"Man, that's irrelevant right now. Is that what happened, or not?"

King looked away in guilt, dreadfully reminded of the child's face that still appeared in his dreams.

"I'm saying, bro," Double-O continued in a disappointed tone, "How come you ain't feel the need to tell me about some shit like that? And say this lil' nigga nine. Which means he old enough to identify some shit."

"Bro, I already knew what you was gon' think. And I have the heart to kill no kid, my baby. So, I was just hoping he was so scared that he wouldn't remember my face."

Massaging the bridge of his nose in frustration, Double-O was thinking about how a team's success largely depended on players sticking to their assigned roles. It was for a reason that Draymond Green shot three-pointers as often as Steph posted up in the paint.

"And you need to holler at your girl, too," Double-O added. "I just found out that nigga Finesse and Dolphin was eating off the same plate. So now I'm wondering if she knew that when she put that play down."

King quickly shook his head in denial, "Nah, bro, she ain't moving like that. She would've at least gave me a heads-up, you feel me?"

"Bro, all I'm saying is holler at her. And at least find out how she even got the nigga number in the first place. Because in case you ain't never heard... they say coincidence is God's way of staying anonymous."

"Fuck that supposed to mean?"

Double-O scoffed, "That it ain't no such thing."

Chapter 15

With an Airpod attached to her left lobe, Mecca carried on a conversation with Kavoni as she jogged on the treadmill in her basement.

"Of course, I've been thinking about you." She smiled, barely winded from the exercise. "You're one of the most persistent men I've ever known. So, how can I not?"

Since revisiting the discussion, she and Kavoni had been having on the day her car broke down, Mecca was finding it increasingly difficult to defend the pressure he was applying. The man didn't let up. And, in addition to her finding Kavoni very attractive, no man had ever pursued her in such a relentless fashion. So, it was kind of cute. But as she had explained to him for umpteenth time, it was somewhat senseless to fall in love with someone whose lifestyle lessened their likelihood of longevity, no matter how enticing.

"So, you gon' let me see you when I get back?" Kavoni asked on the other end, while packing a small, travel bag.

"I'll think about it," Mecca teased. "But you just make sure to be careful."

Pleased by her concern, he joked, "I could always use an extra set of eyes."

"Boy, you know I gotta go to work. You keep talking about how badly I need a new car. So, how you think I'ma get it if I ain't putting these hours in?"

Ending her thirty-minute workout session, Mecca grabbed a towel to erase the beads of sweat from her forehead.

"Speaking of which," she said, "I need to take a quick shower and get ready. But reach out when you get to wherever you going, to let me know you made it."

Kavoni was smiling on his end, knowing his persistence was beginning to pay off. "Yes, ma'am. And why don't you let me rent you a car while I'm gone? Because what you gon' do if that raggedy mu'fucka break down again, and I'm all the way in another state?"

"First off," Mecca laughed, "don't be talking about my wheels like that. Just because your dog get old don't mean you take it out back and put it down. And secondly, I paid that ninja three hundred seventy-four dollars. So, my girl better not be breaking down no time soon."

After they agreed to stay in touch through text messages until his return, Mecca disconnected the call and headed upstairs to the shower, surprised to find herself smiling along the way.

***

With Puma behind the wheel, she and Kavoni were travelling down the interstate in a four-door Mercedes. En route to Milwaukee, Wisconsin, they would soon be meeting with the Hispanic that had introduced Kavoni to contract killing.

After losing his heroin connection, Kavoni knew it was imperative he quickly secure another source of income. His and Puma's savings had taken a substantial loss that he was determined to replenish. So, reaching out to the mediator of his murderous services, he had discreetly explained his need for employment.

Detecting the underlying urgency in Kavoni's tone, the man invited him to his hometown. "And be sure to travel by way of vehicle, as I'm sure you'll enjoy the scenic view along the way."

In essence, he was simply ensuring Kavoni left no evidence of his visit.

Upon their arrival in Milwaukee, the GPS led Puma and Kavoni to a public park in an urban part of the city.

"This must be a serious meeting," Kavoni reasoned, as she backed into a parking space that provided a broad view of the area.

"Why you say that?"

"Because clearly a man like him don't be in places like this."

Puma nodded in understanding. "So, he making sure he ain't seen by nobody he know."

"Exactly."

"But you know what else?" Kavoni added, smiling mischievously.

Her eyes lit up. "What?"

"I gotta feeling whatever it is, we about to earn some serious paper."

Driven by an older man of Spanish descent, a white sedan turned into the park. It slowly circled the lot before making its exit. Moments later, a black-on-black Denali entered the park and reversed into a parking space directly across from the Mercedes.

Along with a tall, slender figure, the Hispanic mediator emerged from the backseat of the armored SUV. Both men in track suits and running shoes, then met up at the front of the vehicle and stopped.

"I got you, my baby," Puma said in assurance, as she removed a micro handgun from inside her boxer briefs.

Kavoni first registered a look of genuine surprise, for he had no idea she had brought a weapon along. Then he frowned, for that was a vibe dissimilar to his own.

"Girl, put that up," he ordered in a scolding tone. "I don't want you to stay in the car, I want you with me."

Excited by her involvement, she quickly replaced the palm-size pistol back in her briefs.

"You didn't mention anything about an accomplice," the mediator stated as Kavoni and Puma walked up.

"Not only do I trust her with my life," Kavoni replied with a direct stare, "but I'd die for her on any given day."

Internally cheesing at his statement, Puma's chin lifted in pride. For she knew Kavoni meant every syllable spoken.

"Well, in that case," the mediator smiled, "let's talk a walk."

With his hands clasped at his back as they leisurely strode along a path of the trash-littered park, the man first informed Kavoni on the manner in which they'd address each other. "From this day forward, I'll be Mr. Brown, and you're Mr. Black. Now, in regard to your request for employment," Mr. Brown continued, "there's a bag of trash I personally need taken out. It'll be heavy, but so will the compensation.'

Kavoni nodded in acceptance. "Say less."

"Then there's a second offer, which is entirely up to you. But I need someone out of state who has the ability to move large quantities of high-grade marijuana. If you're interested, I'll begin you with no less than two hundred pounds."

Although weed sales were not as profitable as hardcore drugs, the quality and quantity would somewhat level out the playing field. *And slow money better than no money*, Kavoni wisely reasoned to himself.

Sealing both deals with a firm handshake, Kavoni assured him that he was fully on board.

As they stood before each other, Mr. Brown calmly spoke, "I saw something special in you from the moment we met in Kentucky. And as I stated then, your savagery is unquestionable. But may you always allow your integrity to be in likeness."

Before parting ways, Kavoni was provided with a set of house keys, where he was told he'd find a small dossier on the target.

As the group was walking to their respective vehicles, Mr. Brown paused to inform Kavoni, "Not that it's mandatory, but if this incident becomes a national subject, I'll double the wages."

Kavoni could hardly contain his excitement as he and Puma reentered the car.

"What I tell you?" he exclaimed, reaching over to playfully palm her head. "We 'bout to go back to the city with at least a hundred grand, plus two hundred pounds of gas."

Grateful to have her best friend back at her side, Puma's heart was filled with a euphoric feeling as she wheeled them out of the park. She had fully regained her confidence and composure, and she was thoroughly convinced she and Kavoni would resume conquering the game.

***

Inside the kitchen of a small house, which was understandably located in the inner city, Kavoni and Puma were reviewing the intel in the dossier. There were a number of photos of the target and his family, along with detailed notes on his daily activities.

"This nigga got more security than the president," Puma commented as she peered at several pictures. "Now I see why he said this shit was gon' be heavy."

Kavoni remained silent as he wore a contemplative expression. He was considering the method in which he could fulfill the contract, without bringing the risk of harm or detainment to either Puma or himself.

As he often did when in deep thought, he rose from the table and began to pace.

Puma observed him with a subtle smile, eagerly awaiting the brilliant idea she knew his mind would soon construct.

When a light of enlightenment suddenly appeared in his eyes, she actually giggled in excitement. "Let me hear it, bro."

He first read over something in the notes, then googled a number before using the house phone to make a brief call.

Upon hanging up, he turned to Puma with devious grin. "Didn't he say he'd double the pay if we made it go national?"

After hearing a rough draft of the plan, Puma had to admit two things, it was bold, but brilliant. And because they both bore mentalities that were fearless by nature, there was no doubt in her mind they could pull it off.

"Bro, that's some movie shit." She smiled. ''And fuck national, they gon' be broadcasting this shit all the way in Ukraine, gotdammit!''

To establish a variety of escape routes, they drove to the site where the killing would take place. Once satisfied they could elude capture should something go wrong, they stopped for takeout before returning to the house.

Later that night, Kavoni moved the refrigerator aside, then lifted two floorboards to reveal a cache of weapons, ranging from rifles to revolvers.

Rubbing her palms together, Puma lit up like a Christmas tree.

"Put your tongue back in your mouth,'' Kavoni teased, "With your lil' thirsty ass.''

For the actual killing itself, they settled on Glock 37's that held .45 caliber rounds. And as reinforcement, just in case the need arose, they'd stash MP-40 submachine guns beneath their seats.

With their hands behind their heads, Puma and Kavoni were quietly laying on a queen-size bed in a darkened room.

Recalling a question he'd been meaning to raise, Kavoni asked Puma how she felt behind Jazz's murder. "Because regardless of what you say, I know you had some type of feelings for her."

"I did," she admitted. "But if I thought Mother Teresa had tried to do you harm, I'd treat her no different. I choose you over everybody, my baby. So, it don't matter how I feel."

Kavoni turned to face her, genuinely proud to have a partner who possessed such an exceptional level of love and loyalty.

When he leaned over to kiss her cheek, he discovered it was damp from a tear that had sneakily trickled from the corner of her eye.

"Come here, girl," he said, pulling Puma into his arms.

As he speaking words of comfort and encouragement in her ear, he realized he had forgotten to notify Mecca of his safe arrival. And had he owned the all-seeing eyesight similar to the Most High's, he would've seen she was worriedly checking her phone every few minutes.

Chapter 16

Two days later...

At a Chuck E. Cheese on the outskirts of Milwaukee, children were ecstatically running throughout the crowded establishment. It was the birthday party of seven-year-old Felix, and his father had ensured that desserts were plentiful.

Along with his wife and two eldest children, the father, Jose, was settled in a corner booth. On the table before them were paper plates of partially eaten birthday cake and ice cream.

Although this was a friendly function, attentively stationed near the front entrance was Jose's favored watchman, who was using a radio to communicate with two mercenaries in a car outside.

A family man to his community and a drug lord to the streets, Jose had recently lowered his cocaine prices in an effort to crush his competitors. While the majority were forced to follow suit or starve, there were others who had collectively decided his move was a mistake, for which he should pay with his life.

Little Felix came running to his father and threw his arms around him. "Daddy, I'm ready for my presents now!"

Jose widened his eyes as if he'd totally forgotten to buy him anything, then shamefully lowered his head and apologized. "I'm so sorry, son. But I honestly forgot."

The seven-year-old eyed his father for a moment, then turned to his mother with a pitiful expression. She had to cover her mouth to stop from laughing.

Before his wife spoiled the joke, Jose laid a hand on his son's shoulder and reassured him, "Don't worry, buddy, I'll make up for it next year. And just think, you'll have twice as many presents."

As the little boy was on the verge of voicing his disappointment, his eyes brightened at the life-size sight of one of his favorite cartoon characters, Sonic the Hedgehog.

"Thank you, Daddy!" He hugged Jose before running off to greet Sonic, who had brought along Sonia.

While the kids were excitedly huddled around the two cartoon characters, Jose shot his wife an inquisitive look. "You arranged that?"

She shook her head. "No, I figured it was one of your surprises."

Warning bells were beginning to ring inside Jose's brain as Sonic playfully bounced toward his booth.

The blue character turned to ruffle a boy's hair, then, when he turned back to face Jose, a firearm had magically appeared in his right hand.

As Jose eyes enlarged in fear and surprise, Sonic the Hedgehog hammered four hollows into Jose's heart.

Due to the chaotic screaming and scrambling of both children and adults, Jose's watchman was unable to get off a clean shot. When he reached to radio for backup, he felt a presence behind him and slowly turned to face the female character, Sonia.

She wagged a shaming finger at him, then fired a round through his forehead, and one beneath his chin as he fell backwards.

Outside in a Chrysler 300, the pair of mercenaries immediately exited the car upon noticing the crowd of people fearfully fleeing from the building. Wired for war, they withdrew their weapons and edged toward the entrance. One of them attempted to radio the watchman, but to no avail.

Using hand signals, they entered the building in a crouched position, prepared to fire.

They first took in their fallen comrade as he floated in a pool of blood, then Jose's wife as she clung to her husband's lifeless corpse.

On pure instinct, one of the men glanced through a window and saw a suspicious-looking van exiting the parking lot.

"There!" He pointed at the vehicle before taking off on foot.

Having shed their costumes, it was indeed Puma and Kavoni inside the white van. And as she was turning out of the parking lot, she glanced at the rearview mirror and saw the two men racing towards a black car.

"Bro, we might got company," she calmly announced.

When Kavoni peered at his side mirror and saw the car speeding in their direction, he donned a pair of shades, then reached beneath his seat and grabbed the MP-40.

"Stop the car," he told Puma, with his hand on the door handle. She complied without hesitation and slammed on the brakes.

Oblivious to traffic as he emerged from the van, Kavoni spun toward the Chrysler and opened fire. With a hundred rounds at his disposal, he managed to easily eliminate the two men.

Hurrying back to the van, he hopped in, and Puma smashed the gas.

Grateful for having gone over various escape routes, they were pulling into a junkyard minutes later.

After changing their attire once again, they splashed gasoline throughout the van and set it afire.

As the interior was engulfed by crackling flames, they casually climbed in the Mercedes and pulled off.

***

"I'm impressed," Mr. Brown praised, as he accompanied Puma and Kavoni along the path of a different park. "And the creativity was so... original."

Labeled "The Animated Assassins," every news station in the state had been broadcasting the barbaric offense. And without a description, motive, or lead, authorities were urging anyone with information to come forward, promising anonymity and a large cash reward.

"As promised," Mr. Brown continued, "the wages will be doubled. And if you'd like, I can arrange for the payment to occur similar to the previous one."

Recalling how his kidnapping had occurred right after receiving the last payment, he insisted on a different method. "Let's just say I had a bad experience last time."

"How so?" Mr. Brown inquired with genuine concern.

Kavoni shook his head. "I'm still here, and that's all that matters."

"Indeed," he replied, then offered to have the money brought to the park, to which Kavoni agreed.

While on the surface it seemed to be a risky move, travelling with a large sum of money was actually something they had prepared for in advance.

"Bro, we on some John Wick and Jason Bourne type shit," Puma joked as they sat inside the car. To avoid unnecessary driving, they had designated the park as the drop off.

"Yeah, we definitely put down a mean demo," Kavoni smirked in recollection. "But not a hair was harmed on a child's head."

"And that's how you get your man." Puma smiled, dapping him up.

As promised, Mr. Brown returned an hour later. Wishing Kavoni a safe trip home, he gave him a firm handshake and a leather satchel filled with Franklins. "I look forward to making you a rich man, my friend."

"So do I." Kavoni grinned. He had no idea that he would soon encounter a mind-blowing surprise.

Before they got back on the road, Puma pulled into a gas station and parked off to the side. She transferred the money to a woman's purse and exited the car.

When she entered the gas station, Kavoni stepped out and acted as if he was a traveler simply stretching his cramped legs. Then, after putting on a convincing show, he went around to the driver's side and climbed in.

Kavoni had to force himself not to laugh as Puma came waddling out of the gas station. Wearing a baby-blue beanie and a sweater that read, *It's A Boy!* She appeared to be around eight months pregnant, by way of a device they had purchased from a costume store, her swollen belly was impregnated with air and two hundred thousand dollars.

Climbing into the passenger seat with caution, just as a pregnant woman would, Puma pinned him with a grim look. "I'm telling you now, bro, I don't even want to hear it."

The seriousness of her expression, combined with the sincerity of her statement caused him to lose it.

Puma glared at him as he laughed uncontrollably, then finally caved in and joined him.

Who would've ever thought the notorious Puma would be playing the role of a pregnant woman!

Fumiya Payne

Chapter 17

"Nigga, I'm done with this shit!" Unique yelled as she was throwing clothes into a Louis Vuitton suitcase. "I should've better than to be fooling around with some little-ass boy!"

"Oh, so now I'm a boy just because I asked you a question?" King replied in disbelief.

"There's some shit you shouldn't have to ask. Especially not after all I've done for your ungrateful ass."

The couple had been soaking in the bathtub, when he questioned her in regard to whether or not she'd known about the connection between Dolphin and Finesse. Craning her neck to look back, she had asked him if he was serious. King had flashed a nervous grin and said it was just something one of his men had wanted him to ask. Unique had then angrily risen from the tub and without drying off, stormed out of the bathroom.

"You can't be serious," King said as she was zipping the case closed. "I'm saying, you really about to leave just because I asked you a fucking question?"

"Like I said, there's some shit you shouldn't have to ask. And when you do, it comes off like an accusation. That's like me asking you if you ever fucked around with a dude before. How the fuck would take that?"

When he didn't respond, she replied, "Exactly."

As she went to walk by him, King grabbed her arm.

"Nigga, if you don't let go of me…"

"I'm saying, I do everything you ask me to do. I fuck how you tell me to fuck. I listen to all your advice, and I confide in you about shit I don't even share with Double-O. So, you can't just stand here and act like that don't count for nothing."

"King, I told you from the jump I wouldn't tolerate you allowing people to interfere with our relationship. And I stand by that."

"The nigga just wanted me to ask you a question. That's it. And it ain't like he knows your character like I do. So how can you really expect him to not be concerned or curious about some shit? And this the same nigga that would die for me in a heartbeat. So, if he ask me to ask you a simple-ass question, I owe that man that."

"Yeah, well," she said averting her gaze, "I'm not about to be competing for no nigga's devotion."

"It ain't even about that, Unique. It's about you understanding you're not the only one on this earth who got my best interests at heart."

King recalled something Kavoni once said and added, "They say if you want to go fast... go alone. But if you want to far... go together."

"I don't care about none of that!" she shouted. "My only concern is me and you. Everything and everybody else is irrelevant. Period, point, muthafucking blank. And if you can't accept that, then this shit is a waste of time."

"But that's the only real friend I got. He ain't never been nothing but loyal. And he ain't never spoke one bad word about you. So, I don't understand where all this hostility coming from."

Unique scoffed in disgust. "Yeah, let's see how far you get without me. And let's see if your friend can give you that family you always talk about."

King frowned as she was walking away. "What's that supposed to mean?"

Pausing in the doorway, Unique reached in her purse to remove two slender items, one of which she tossed on the floor.

"See you around, King," she said before exiting the bedroom.

Walking over to what she had thrown on the floor, King bent to pick it up and couldn't believe his eyes. For in his palm was a pregnancy stick that read, "positive."

***

Inside the red Durango, Double-O turned down a west side street known for being heavily patrolled by prostitutes. Unbeknownst to King, or any of his other comrades, this was the manner in he fulfilled his lower desires. For it came with a varied selection and no attachment.

Halfway down the block he took notice of a voluptuous woman with blonde hair. The fact that she wore shades at night was intriguing enough to make him pull over and partially lower the passenger window.

"What up, doe?" he called out.

Slightly bending at the waist, the woman attempted to make out his face. "I don't know, you tell me."

"I got one rubber and five hunnid!"

"You po-po?" she quickly inquired, thinking his proposition was too good to be true.

Double-O smirked, "By no means. But I am in a hurry."

Knowing police officers had to identify themselves if questioned, the woman practically sprinted to the passenger window. After she first ensure that he didn't resemble a creep, she'd then get in and guarantee him a memorable experience.

As she leaned down to peer inside, she opened her mouth to speak, but instead released a loud gasp.

Double-O frowned at her reaction, yet to make the connection.

"Little Marjuan," she said in a near whisper, then removed the large shades.

Time seemed to stop as he eyed the woman in disbelief. In spite of the purplish bruise beneath her right eye, he recognized the face of someone he had hoped to never see again... his mother's.

Impregnated at the age of fifteen, Tina Brunson had not only been clueless of the correct way to raise a child, but she lacked any desire to learn. She would've had an abortion, if not for a desperate attempt to entrap the father. But once he made it clear that he wanted no dealings with her, or a child he denied as being his, rejection soon led to the resentment of her own infant.

Raised in a household where discipline was served for dinner, Tina had brought her son up on the same strict diet. Whether he cooed or cried, she'd beat him to sleep. And how he survived was a mystery to all those who had known of the abuse.

But as Marjuan grew older and his heart got colder, he would bring the torture to a close shortly after his eleventh birthday. One night, Tina had attempted to assault him with a table leg, which he wrestled away and backed her into a corner. "If you ever try to hurt me again, I'ma strangle you. And if you try to get me locked up, when I get out, I'm still gon' strangle you. Now nod that head if you understand."

As Tina had stared into the eyes of the monster she created, she wisely nodded her head in consent. And before Marjuan would befriend King months later and run away, the only meals Tina served were those from a stove.

After recovering from the shock of seeing her only child for the first time in nearly nine years, Tine smiled at his appearance. "You look to be doing pretty good for yourself."

Maintaining a solemn expression, Double-O shrugged. "Better than some, worse than others."

Tina looked down and nodded, as if his coldness was understandable. For she'd been a terrible mother, a fact she could neither deny nor erase. But as a woman who'd been forced to lug around the weight of regret, she could do the right thing for once in her life.

"Marjuan, I know there's nothing I can say that'll change the past, but I do want to say I'm very sorry. And that's from the bottom of my worthless heart. I don't ever expect you to forgive me or offer me a second chance at being a mother. But I do hope you don't make the same mistake I made, which was taking the anger I had for one person out on another."

As the precision of her statement resonated within Double-O's mind, he thought about his fear and inability to form emotional attachments with women. He clung to the belief that if he could be mistreated by the very woman who carried him in her womb for nine months, then surely another woman wouldn't hesitate to play hockey with his heart.

"Aye, yo, I'm about to slide," Double-O said, readjusting himself in the seat. "But just so you know, I don't hold no hard feelings toward you. Because at least you ain't put me in no microwave, you feel me."

As Tina searched for what to say in farewell, he reached in his pocket and pulled out a bankroll.

"I don't know how far this gon' take you," he said, leaning over to hand her the money, "but it's all I got on me right now."

Staring at what was well over his initial offering of five hundred dollars, Tina desperately needed it, but knew she didn't deserve it.

"Baby, as much as I want to, I can't accept that. Because it would like excusing everything I did, and that's something I gotta take up with God when I meet Him."

In the gentlest gesture she'd ever shown him, Tina reached out to cover her son's hand. "I'm just grateful for the chance to say how sorry I am, Marjuan. I've prayed and waited for this moment for a long time. And it means more to me than any amount of money. So, you be careful out here, baby. And please try to find mercy in your heart. And not for me, but others."

Swallowing a lump in his throat, Double-O had to turn away. He hadn't dropped a tear in years but knew he'd do so if he didn't quickly drive off. While she had hurt him in every sense, she was still his mother. And the sincerity in which she'd spoken, coupled with her present appearance and situation, was beginning to soften his hardened heart.

"Like I said," he spoke without looking at her, "I gotta move around. But you be careful out here as well."

As Tina stepped away from the vehicle, Double-O tossed the money out the window and sped off.

When he paused at a stop sign and peeked at his rearview mirror, he had to force himself not to blink, for the tears in his eyes would've surely escaped.

As he merged into traffic on a main street, Double-O's thoughts were no longer centered on sex, but on savagery.

"Somebody gotta feel my pain," he growled, gripping a full-sized Glock.

Fumiya Payne

Chapter 18

Safely arriving back in Detroit, Kavoni and Puma's first stop was to a storage unit. While the staircase had been a brilliant idea, returning their earnings to a compromised location was a risk they were unwilling to take.

After placing the majority of the money in a medium-size safe, they thoroughly cleaned the AMG's interior and returned it to the rental agency.

As they were walking across the parking lot, Kavoni still shook his head in amusement at Puma's new car. When she said she had something in mind, he never thought it would resemble something from a mafia movie.

On twenty-inch wire wheels and gangster white walls, Puma was pushing a 1969 Cadillac Sedan DeVille. With a flawless dark-mauve paint job and matching interior, it was topped off with an original alligator-printed vinyl roof.

Puma slid her small stature behind the wheel of the limo-sized slab and brought its engine to life. Then, before pulling off she cut on a song that made Kavoni smile, for it was one of their favorites by the late rapper, DMX.

"Now who I am is who I'll be until I die, either accept it or don't fuck with it/ but if we gon' be dawgs, then you stuck with it/ Let me go my way, but walk with me/ see what I see, watch me, then talk with me/ Share my pain, make it a lil' easier deal with/ because despite all the fame, you I'ma keep it real with/ rob and steal with..."Arriving at Puma's house, she and Kavoni went inside to be greeted by an energetic Squeeze and a smiling Shawna.

"What's up with all that?" she laughed, pointing at Puma's attire.

"Girl, it's a long story," she said, pulling off the beanie.

After giving Puma a hug and promising to call her as soon as he got home, Kavoni kissed Shawna's cheek and he and Squeeze made their exit.

No sooner than he pulled off did he phone Mecca, who answered on the second ring.

"Damn,'' he teasingly said, "You snatched that mu'fucka up like you was waiting right by it, or something."

"You wish."

"I'm saying, if you thirsty for a nigga, just let me know and I'll come quench that lil' shit."

"Whatever," Mecca laughed. "Ain't nobody thirsty to see you, boy. And besides, you on restrictions, anyway. Don't think I forgot."

After failing to notify Mecca of him safely arriving in Milwaukee, she had threatened to terminate all further contact. "I understand you might have a lot going on in your life, but that doesn't excuse you not standing by your word, Kavoni. I'm big on that. So, I'm asking you not to let this happen again."

Assuring her it was a mistake he doesn't usually make, he promised to right his wrongs upon his return to the city. Which was what he now planned to do.

"But I'm saying,'' Kavoni said into the phone, "if I'm on restrictions, then how I'ma right my wrong like I said I would? Because I know you ain't gon' force me to foul out."

"Listen at you, trying to be all convincing and stuff."

"I'm just saying."

"Yeah, well, I don't get off work for another two hours."

"That's perfect. Because I just got back, and that'll give me time to drop Squeeze off and take a shower real quick."

"Nah, you don't gotta drop Squeeze off. I want to meet him."

"You want to meet him?"

"Did I stutter?"

"But I'm saying, I thought we was just gon' chill. You know, watch a movie, or something."

"We can. But that ain't got nothing to do with you bringing the dog. It ain't like he gon' be in the way."

Kavoni chuckled, "Yeah, you right."

Quick on her toes, Mecca replied, "Oh, what you thought you was coming over here to act mannish?"

He laughed again, "Nah, I ain't say that."

"Alright, well bring the dog with you, then. And I'll see you at my house in two hours."

When he disconnected the call, Kavoni looked over at Squeeze and said in a serious tone, "Bra, we gon' let her pet you and play with you for a lil' bit, then I'ma need you to take your cool ass to sleep."

***

With a picture of King they'd gotten off social media, Dolphin and Nooni were en route to the new house where Finesse's baby mother and child now lived. Unsure if the boy would identify King or not, Dolphin was submerged in a sea of suspense.

Turning down the street on which the house was located, both men registered shocked expressions at the scene before them.

The front of the house was roped off with crime scene tape, as the area crawled with law enforcement and EMT's. Due to the excessive number of squad cars and other emergency vehicles, Nooni could only get within a certain distance of the house.

"What you want to do?" he asked, unable to drive any closer.

Dolphin was considering his answer, when he spotted an EMT ducked off behind an ambulance, furiously sucking on a cancer stick.

"I'll be right back," he said before hopping out.

When the man looked up and saw Dolphin approaching him, he quickly dropped the cigarette and crushed it with the sole of his shoe.

"Tell me what happened, and I won't rat you out," Dolphin said in a joking manner.

The man lowered his head and shook it. "Trust me, you don't want to know."

"Nah, actually I do," Dolphin replied in a more serious tone. "My nephew live in there. So at least tell me he alright."

He looked at Dolphin with a remorseful expression, "Man, I wish I could."

Dolphin listened in disbelief as the EMT gave a description of the gruesome discovery. "I've seen a lot on the job, but nothing like that."

Fumiya Payne

Wearing a grave expression as he reentered the car, Dolphin just sat there, staring off into space.

"What he say?" Nooni inquired before reversing down the block.

"Bro, we dealing with some real live animals," he mumbled. "He said they found both bodies, face down on the bedroom floor. And they both had two bullets in the back of their heads."

"Damn," was all Nooni could say in response.

Dolphin turned to him with a deeply disturbed look and added, "Bro, he said they was holding hands. So that means they knew it was coming. And I can only imagine the fear they felt."

Dolphin shuddered as he envisioned the emotional exchange that likely occurred during their final moments. And to think he had just spoken to Keisha last night and said he'd swing by the following afternoon to show her son the picture.

The two men were riding in silence, when Dolphin suddenly looked at Nooni and said, "Bro, I need you to promise me something."

He briefly removed his eyes from the road and replied, "Anything."

"I need you to promise that if something ever happen to me, you'll personally get Teeka and her mama as far away from here as possible. Don't let nothing happen to my baby, Nooni."

"I promise I wouldn't do nothing less," he assured Dolphin in his sincerest tone. "The same way I'd die for you, is the same thing I'd do for that lil' girl."

Had Dolphin been able to predict the future, he would've known that Nooni had just made a promise he'd be unable to keep.

104

Chapter 19

It was love at first sight when Mecca and Squeeze met. And since his and Kavoni's arrival to her house, the dog had yet to leave her side. It touched her heart to hear how he had lost one of his eyes as a puppy and made her love him just that much more.

"If I didn't know any better," Mecca teasingly said while giving Squeeze a belly-rub, "I'd say old Squeeze would pick me over you."

"And I'd drop his ass off back where I found him," Kavoni laughed.

"Oh, no you wouldn't!" she objected. "Because we'd jump you. Ain't that right, boy?''

With his massive head in her lap, Squeeze looked up and tried to lick her face.

Mecca moved away, laughing. "You my boy and all, but we ain't doing no kissing."

Having a sudden thought, she moved Squeeze aside and went into the kitchen. She returned seconds later with a glazed honeybun.

As Squeeze keyed in on her hand in anticipation, Kavoni intervened. "He can't have that.''

"Why not?"

"He just can't."

"It's only a treat, Kavoni. It ain't like he gon' be eating 'em every day."

Her words falling on deaf ears, Kavoni slapped his thigh and barked, "Squeeze, here!"

Complying without hesitation, the dog jumped down from the couch and went to join Kavoni at his left side.

"So, you really just gon' ruin my moment?" Mecca said in persistence.

"It ain't about ruining no moment, it's about me sticking to his diet plan."

Kavoni had recently reached back out to his dog handler, Malloyd, and informed him of his desire to get Squeeze inside the box. Whether it was killing, dealing, or dog fighting, Kavoni had every intention on increasing his crops. And he refused to let something as simple as a honeybun hinder the harvest. But, of course, he couldn't explain all this to Mecca.

"A diet plan?" Mecca repeated, refusing to deaden the conversation. "He don't look to be overweight to me. And I'ma nurse, so I would definitely know."

"Why you being so adamant about this?"

"Why you being so evasive with your answer? Kavoni smirked. "So, you really not gon' let this go, huh?"

Mecca folded her arms in defiance. "So, you really not gon' answer my question, huh?"

With Mecca already frowning upon his illicit lifestyle, he could only imagine how she'd respond if she found out he was also involved in the brutal sport of dog fighting. Especially after the apparent connection she and the dog had already established. This had been the main reason for him postponing the introduction.

"Mecca, listen, I don't—"

"Don't even worry about it, Kavoni." She waved her hand. "I'm over it. But look, it's getting late, and I gotta go to work tomorrow. So, I'ma call it a night.''

Kavoni rose up from the couch. "You know, it's a lot of people who've missed out on their blessings behind the most trivial things. It's like, when shit don't go perfect, or exactly how they want it, they just assume it's meant to be and give up. Not knowing some shit require a little more time and effort."

"What you're saying makes sense," Mecca replied. "But, in this instance, it doesn't apply. But since you call yourself putting me up on game, allow me to return the favor. Because what it boils down to is this… most men think all women are the same. And in reality, that's as close to the truth as the earth is to the sun."

"I don't think all the women—"

"Kavoni, you may not think it, but your actions imply it. And you know what else your actions imply... that you're selfish."

"I ain't never been selfish," he sternly remarked. "I'd give my last to see a loved one happy.''

"I'm speaking on a much deeper level than materialism, Kavoni. But that's exactly my point. Because how many times have I told

106

you I've felt pain I can't even describe, and don't wish to willingly experience that feeling again? But you could care less about any of that, as long as Kavoni gets what he wants. If you weren't selfish, you'd take my feelings into consideration. Because we both know you can't promise me, you'll return home from those streets every night. And I can't promise you I'll show up to a visiting room for the next twenty years.

"Kavoni, you gotta understand, every woman's heart can't be bought by a man's bank account or good looks. There are some of us who require a connection that goes deeper than what's on the surface. One that involves compromise and unquestionable loyalty. And how can a man claim he's willing to offer either of those, if he can't even stay out of jail? Because I'm sorry, sweetie, but you can't say you love me in one breath, then turn around and leave me out here to fend for myself in the next. A real man, who's really ready to love will compromise for a real woman. Period. And until he's prepared to make certain sacrifices, then he gotta respect that woman's decision to safeguard her heart."

Mecca's speech left him momentarily speechless. She was not only the most beautiful woman he'd ever known, but she was by far the deepest.

Damn, I ain't never thought about it like that," Kavoni humbly admitted. "And I can't dispute none of what you said. But I can say that since we've been talking, I've been having thoughts that I ain't never had before. It's like, a nigga get so caught up in this street shit that it becomes normal. But then I guess the right person can come along and point out the error in a nigga's thinking, you feel me. Because you done opened me up to some different shit. Got me thinking like, what joy is in life if it's absent of love?"

Regarding him in understanding, Mecca walked over to him and grabbed his hand. "You've been through a lot yourself, Kavoni. And we've both witnessed how determined you are to survive. But, instead of seeing that experience as a symbol that you're invincible, you should hear it as a message that's telling you to make the most out of life while you still have it. Because tomorrow ain't promised, and you don't want to take your last breath in a wishful state. Wishing you had did this or wishing you would've done that."

Kavoni could only smile in amazement at her thinking process. It wasn't often a man stumbled across a young woman with such wisdom.

"Mecca, as the Most High is my witness," Kavoni said, raising his right hand, "I knew you was something different from the moment I met you. But the more I get to know you, the more I realize I really didn't have a clue on how special you truly are."

Smiling in appreciation of his praise, she gave him a hug. "That was sweet of you, Kavoni. I knew there was a gentleman beneath all that gangsterism."

Intoxicated by the fragrance of her hair and skin, he tightly enclosed his arms around her waist. "Mmm, you smell so good."

"Kavoni, I know you didn't bring no gun in my house."

He smiled. "Nah, why you say that?"

"Because that's what it feel like poking me in my stomach right now."

"Don't worry, love," he jokingly assured her, "because that gun don't shoot bullets."

"Boy, let me go!" she laughed, pressing her hands on his chest to pry herself loose. "That thing ain't even been registered."

Releasing her in reluctance, Kavoni peered deeply into her pupils and pronounced, "I have genuine feelings for you, Mecca. I mean, unlike anything I've ever felt for any other woman. I ain't never thought about settling down, until I met you. So, I'm asking that you don't give up on me just yet. I'ma man with many faults but mistreating a woman ain't one of 'em. And I give you my word, I just need one year and I'ma cut off all ties to the streets. And in return for your patience, I'll dedicate the rest of my life to making you happy."

"Why are you making this so hard for me?" she asked, dropping her head in frustration. "Why are you so insistent on breaking my heart?"

"That's not what I'm trying to do at all, Mecca. I just want to make sure that money is never an issue. As a man, I want to be able to properly take care of my woman. I don't want to have to ever deny you something because I can't afford it."

"But I don't need a bunch of money or clothes to make me happy. If you want to properly take care of me, then love me unconditionally. Be loyal to me. Treat me with the respect you'd treat your mother with. And if you could do those things, then it wouldn't matter if we was living in a shack out in the middle of the woods."

"I hear everything you saying. I do. And it's cool that you're not a materialistic woman. But I'm only asking for one year. And whether I'm up a million or down a billion, I'm done."

Before giving her a chance to reply with another one of her witty remarks, Kavoni reached in his jacket and removed a purple jewelry case, which just so happened to be her favorite color.

When he opened the case, Mecca gasped at the sight of a Cartier necklace, accompanied by a heart-shaped pendant with purple diamonds.

"I'll never break your heart," he said, placing the necklace around her neck.

Smitten with joy at the most beautiful gift she'd ever received, Mecca looked up at him with a tearful expression. "Kavoni, I love it. But you shouldn't have."

"This only the beginning," he replied, thinking of how her emotional reaction made the purchase worth every cent spent.

Before leaving, Kavoni kissed her cheek and urged her to consider his proposal. "Just one year, love. That's all I need."

Promising she'd sleep on it, Mecca reminded him to call her the moment he stepped foot through his front door.

As Kavoni tapped the horn twice and sped off, there was a warm, tingly feeling coursing throughout his entire body. Unlike anything he'd ever experienced, it was a feeling to which he could grow accustomed. But he knew he'd first have to make some ultimate sacrifices.

Speeding down the interstate, Kavoni was nearing his exit, when he received a call from Malloyd.

"What's good, OG?" he respectfully greeted.

"What's going on, young bull, how you feeling?"

"Hungry."

"Well, in that case, I got good news. I was able to do what you asked. But there's one thing."

"Talk to me."

"Some joker paid the forfeit fee and backed out the match. So, if you step up, it's scheduled for the end of next month. That's forty-two days and a wake.''

"Damn!" Kavoni grunted to himself. He had faith in his boy, but to have him scratch on such short notice could be detrimental to his wealth, and the dog's health.

"What the pot like?" Kavoni inquired.

"Shit, buddy saying no less than seventy-five. He gotta all-white grand champ named Hitler. Me personally, I don't know if your boy ready, but I'm just doing what you asked me to."

If they were to attain victory, Kavoni would not only be able to add another hundred and fifty grand to his savings, but Squeeze would have defeated a grand champ. And the challenges that would pour in afterwards would surely place them on the path to prominence.

Telling Malloyd that he was all in, Kavoni was grateful for refusing Squeeze that honeybun. Because with only forty-two days to prepare for battle, there was no room for error or laxity. And a dog's diet prior to an upcoming match was crucial.

As he exited the E-way, Kavoni glanced over at Squeeze, who was already watching him.

"We soldiers, my baby," he reasoned with the dog. "And it's time to go to war."

Chapter 20

Martha was attached to Puma's right hand as she and Shawna stood in a wooded area. Placed on top of a table twenty yards away were four coffee cans.

With Shawna paying close attention, Puma extended the weapon in both hands, relaxed her breathing and put a bullet in each can.

Shawna smiled, genuinely impressed by her marksmanship. "You make it look so easy, Puma."

"You will, too," she replied, picking up the spent casings and placing them inside her backpack.

After lining the cans back on the table, Puma handed the gun to Shawna. "Your turn."

While certain people would frown upon some of Puma's parenting techniques, she was simply showing the girl the most effective way of protecting herself. As victims of sexual abuse, they had firsthand experience with the feeling of being powerless. So, to ensure Shawna had a fighting chance in a world where mercy was rarely extended, Puma would teach her the art of self-defense.

As Shawna was handling the gun, she happened to notice a series of nicks along its slide.

"Puma, what's all these marks?" she asked, counting a total of six.

"Let's just stay focused for right now," she answered. "And maybe that's something we'll discuss down the road."

While Puma was certain her secret would be safe with Shawna, she didn't think the girl was ready to learn that the number of marks represented the amount of kills she'd committed with Martha alone.

When Shawna raised the gun in both hands, Puma stepped behind her. "You see those two little things at the top?"

Shawna nodded.

"Well, if you look between 'em before you shoot, it'll help with your aim. So, think of one of them cans as a nigga's head. And aim for the center, right between his eyes."

Flinching at the discharge, Shawna fired and missed either can.

"Just relax," Puma encouraged her. "This ain't no test. This all about survival. Plus, we got all day and a box of bullets.''

Shawna missed the next three shots and lowered the firearm in frustration. "I can't do it."

Puma grabbed her by the arm and roughly spun her around. "It's been paralyzed people who willed themselves to walk again. So don't ever let me hear you say what you can't do. Now turn your ass back around and keep trying."

Realigning the weapon with one of the cans, she took a deep breath and slowly exhaled. Then, staring down the sights as Puma had instructed, she calmly squeezed the trigger.

At the sight of a can flying off the table, she turned to Puma and squealed in triumph. "I did it!"

"You did." Puma smiled. "Now do it again."

Over the next hour, Shawna would gain better aim and more confidence. And when it was time to leave, Puma would have to nearly wrestle the gun from the girl's grasp, as she was now addicted to the feeling of power the weapon provided. She'd been victimized on various levels throughout her entire life, and it felt so good to finally be on the other end, even she was only killing cans.

"We'll come back next weekend," Puma promised. "And I might even bring something a lil' bigger.''

"Like what?" Shawna eagerly inquired.

"I don't know," she playfully shrugged, "Maybe like a Mac-11, or something.''

When her eyes lit up like fireworks, Puma laughed. "Girl, let me find out you on some Lara Croft shit for real."

After removing the cans from the table and placing them in a small trash bag, Puma pointed toward a nearby tree and asked Shawna if there was anything memorable about it.

She eyed it for a minute before replying, "Yeah, it got that hole at the bottom of it. Like squirrels or something be living in there.''

Proud of Shawna's perceptive eye, Puma had her stand directly in front of the tree, then backpedal exactly five steps.

"Stay right there and don't move," she instructed Shawna before jogging back to the car.

She returned a minute later carrying a small shovel.

Looking over her shoulder, Shawna wore an inquisitive look as Puma forced the blade into a patch of dirt behind her and started digging. "What's going on, Puma?"

"Preparation," she answered, continuing to dig.

After digging several feet into the ground, Puma laid the shovel aside, then withdrew a brick-shaped package from her backpack.

"This fifty thousand," she informed Shawna, holding up the package. "I don't plan on dying anytime soon, but shit happens. So, in the event that I ain't here no more, this is so you'll have something to fall back on."

Having been around Shawna long enough to know when she was on the verge of becoming emotional, Puma pointed a disapproving finger at her. "Girl, don't start that."

"It's just, I was all by myself before you came along. I didn't have nobody. And I don't know what you see in me, but you the first person to ever love me. And I doubt I'll ever meet somebody else who'll care about me. So, I don't know what I'd do without you, Puma."

That girl really knew how to pluck at the sentimental strings of Puma's heart. She was so naive and innocent, any decent human being would only want to love and protect her.

As Puma was replacing the dirt over the hole, she recalled her and Kavoni's recent discussion in regard to retirement. While she had never considered living a life outside of wrongdoing, Shawna's presence had managed to provide her with a sense of purpose. So, while she had initially been unsure about the idea of migrating to a foreign region, she knew it would likely be in the girl's best interest.

Once the dirt was back intact, Puma advised Shawna on the easiest way to remember the location of the burial site. "Five steps from the hole and turn."

They were walking back to the car, when Shawna looked at Puma as if she wanted to say something, then looked away.

"What's on your mind?" Puma asked, having noticed the look out the corner of her eye.

Shawna hesitated before asking, "If your lifestyle is so danger-ous, then why do you keep living it?"

Struck by the sensibleness of her question, Puma smiled. "Girl, you sure you ain't never been here before?"

"Been where?"

Puma shook her head in amusement, "Nah, it's just a figure of speech. But to answer your question... this lifestyle is all I've ever known. I ain't justifying it, but I was placed in a sink-or-swim situ-ation, and I chose to swim. Had I been taught different, or raised different, then I'm sure I would've turned out different. But these the cards I was dealt. And instead of complaining about having a bad hand, I make the most of it. Just as I'm sure you'll do the same if something was to happen to me."

"But I'm not as tough as you."

Puma nodded, "Yeah, you is. You've just never had nobody point it out to you. Just like earlier, when you thought you couldn't hit that can. I convinced you that you could, and then you did it. And it's like that with everything else in life. We just happen to be the underdogs, my baby. So, that just mean we gotta walk a little farther and fight a little harder."

"But trust me, Shawna," Puma added, as they approached the trunk of her car, "I might not be around to see it, but one day you gon' shed that cocoon and blossom into a beautiful butterfly."

Chapter 21

After dropping Squeeze off with Malloyd, whom he instructed to push the dog to his limit, Kavoni met up with his crew behind a vacant apartment building owned by Dolphin.

"What up, brodie?" Puma greeted, the first to give Kavoni a hug and handshake.

Exchanging embraces with Dolphin, Nooni, and a handful of other hooligans, Kavoni began to inform them on how the afternoon would unfold. "We gon' keep two men on the roof, facing opposite directions. It's probably gon' be a minute, but you'll need to stay focused and patient. And if you see anybody come through that look suspicious, fire their ass straight up. And that'll be all the warning the rest of them will need.''

Dolphin selected his top two shooters. "You niggas don't miss. So, I'ma need y'all to hold it down. And I'ma hit y'all mitts with something real decent.''

Dolphin had been genuinely pleased and relieved upon learning of Kavoni's survival. There had also been a significant rise in his level of respect, for it required a certain caliber of man to withstand and endure a tortuous kidnapping. So, if there had been any prior uncertainty in Kavoni's ability to lead, his death-defying deed had dissolved all doubt. Needless to say, Dolphin had readily accepted his invitation into the weed industry.

Once the two heavily armed men were planted on the roof, Kavoni and the others went to post up on the building's front porch.

As they were recapping the plays of a recent Piston's game, a furniture truck turned down their street. Dolphin placed two fingers in his mouth and whistled, signaling for his men on the roof to be alert.

Descending the porch as the truck grew closer, Kavoni stood near the curb and removed his hat. Any other gesture and the driver would've rolled past.

Parking in the middle of the street, the driver activated his hazard lights and climbed out.

Fumiya Payne

"Good afternoon, sir," the older man pleasantly greeted. "Would you happen to be Mr. Black?"

"I am," Kavoni replied. "And brown my favorite color."

"Well, let's get you your furniture," he said, winking his eye in amusement at their coded game.

Waving for the others to join, Kavoni followed the man to back of the truck, where he raised its door to reveal a couch, two dressers, and a king-size mattress.

As the truck was being unloaded, the man produced an invoice and requested Mr. Black's signature. "Gotta make it look good."

Kavoni scribbled something impossible to read and gripped the man's hand in a firm shake. "Safe travels."

"I'll do my best." He smiled. "And you be sure to enjoy that mattress. It's one of the softest our store offers."

Inside the basement of the apartment building, where they'd laid the mattress beside a bathtub, everyone stood around in suspense as Kavoni removed the plastic.

When he used a knife to cut the middle seam from head-to-foot, they stared in awe as the mattress opened up to expose vacuum-sealed bags of marijuana. Ranging from OG Kush to other potent strands with outlandish names, they would soon learn that there were actually two hundred and fifty compressed pounds.

With everyone working in union, they were opening up the bags and dumping the weed into the tub. From there they would bag up various amounts for distribution. And until they had the city sown up, they agreed not to sell anything over a quarter pound.

"Nigga, this shit reeking!" Puma laughed, as the tub was nearly full.

"I hope ain't none of y'all on probation," another man joked, "Cause you gon' piss dirty off just the smell alone!"

Kavoni had opened one of the bags and was dumping it out, when a square-shaped package fell into the tub.

It was almost comedic the way everyone took notice of it and immediately stopped what they were doing. And they'd all had been in the streets since childhood, so it was no mystery that they were looking at a kilo of something.

116

"Is that what I think it is?" Puma said without removing her eyes from it.

Reaching into the tub, Kavoni picked up the package and tested its weight. It certainly felt like a thousand grams. But there was only way to find out.

He grabbed the knife, jabbed it into the top of the package and carefully withdrew it. There was a tan substance along the tip of the blade. He looked at Puma, then turned back to the knife and extended his tongue.

Kavoni made a sour face at the taste of what he now knew to be pure heroin. His reaction only heightened everyone's excitement.

Puma had a sudden thought and shared it. "Bro, what if there's more?"

Upon further examination, they would surprisingly discover five more kilos. And with each of them likely bearing the same level of purity as the first one, they could easily convert the six into eighteen.

As Kavoni's mind raced in a number of directions, he concluded that the old man had likely given him the wrong furniture. Because Mr. Brown had never mentioned anything about the inclusion of heroin.

"Bro, that old dude fucked up," Puma said, thinking along the same lines as Kavoni. "He done gave us the wrong shit."

Kavoni stood up from the tub and rubbed a hand over his face.

"What you thinking, my baby?" Dolphin inquired.

Peering around at his people, Kavoni knew they had already done the math on six bricks of pure. He knew because he'd conducted the same calculations. And there was a large margin between heroin and weed sales.

"I'm thinking like Puma," he answered. "The old man fucked up. And we talking about six bricks of pure. So, we know the numbers. But at the same time, my character has always been unquestionable. And I'm not gon' let no amount of money change that. So, while the greed in me want to keep it, the real in me won't allow it."

While Puma could detect disappointment on a few of their disheartened faces, she could've never been prouder of her best friend's decision. For he refuted the validity of the saying, "There is no honor amongst thieves."

Excusing himself from the basement, Kavoni stepped outside to make a phone call.

"Hello?" Mr. Brown answered on the other end.

"This Mr. Black, sir."

"Good afternoon, Mr. Black. I'm assuming everything went well with the delivery of your furniture."

"It did. But there were six lamps in there that I didn't order. So, I wasn't sure if the order got mixed up, or what."

Mr. Brown chuckled on the other end. "No, there was no mix up. Those were intended for you, my friend. And because you were honest enough to bring it to my attention, I'll make sure to send you twice as many whenever you're ready."

Elated beyond his wildest dreams, Kavoni felt like he was walking on air as he returned to the basement. *And who say it don't pay to be real?* he thought.

"What he say?" Puma anxiously inquired as he reentered the basement.

"It was a test!" Kavoni smiled. "He just wanted to see what I was gon' do."

He picked Puma up and swung her around as if she was a little girl. "We back, my baby, we back!"

***

Kavoni parked in front of a white house that had a "for sale" sign planted in the yard. This was a visit he'd been meaning to make, but somehow it had always seemed to slip his mind. Well, not today. So, though he hadn't called ahead, he was hoping the person was home.

Approaching the house, he was on the verge of knocking, when the front door was suddenly opened.

"Whatever you selling, I ain't buying," an elderly woman barked from behind the screen door.

Kavoni smiled. "I'm not here to sell anything, ma'am. My name Kavoni McClain, and I was locked up with your son, Freddie. I don't know if he ever mentioned me or not, but I told him if I ever made it, so would he. And I'm just here to honor my word."

Freddie-D had indeed mentioned Kavoni's name to his mother on a number of occasions, but that didn't prevent her from requesting to see his identification. "You say you Kavoni, but until I see some type of proof, I don't believe you."

Respectful of her cautious nature, though he was inwardly amused, Kavoni removed his I.D. and held it up to the glass. After a thorough inspection, she unlocked the screen door and invited him in.

"Boy, if you don't give me a hug," Mrs. Daniels warned. "The way my Freddie talk about you, you'd think you was my youngest boy."

She offered refreshments, which Kavoni declined. "I can't stay long, ma'am. But I've learned firsthand that tomorrow ain't promised, so this is something I had to make sure I took care of."

With that said, he removed an envelope from the inner pocket of his coat and held it out to her. "This enough for Freddie's lawyer, and whatever else he need."

Eyeing the envelope in disbelief, the woman raised a trembling hand to her mouth and mumbled a prayer of gratitude to her heavenly Father. For her son was scheduled to go before the parole board in a matter of months, and she'd had no idea on how she would come up with the lawyer's money. Which explained the "for sale" sign out in the front yard. She'd been willing to sell her home for the sake of her son's freedom.

Offering Kavoni another hug and sincere words of appreciation, she promised to include him in her daily prayers.

"Thank you, ma'am, I could really use it."

Something dawned on Kavoni as he was turning to leave, and he told Mrs. Daniels to hold on and he'd right back.

She watched in curiosity as he opened his trunk, busied himself with something inside, then came jogging back to the house.

Partially stepping inside the screen door, Kavoni reached in his coat and pulled out a large wad of loose bills.

"I don't know exactly how much this is," he explained to the wide-eyed woman, "But I hope it's enough to take care of whatever bills you might have."

Kavoni kissed her cheek and promised to return sometime in the near future. On his way to the car, he snatched the sign out the ground and took it with him.

After watching Kavoni drive off, Mrs. Daniels rolled her teary eyes upwards and again thanked her Creator. Because a stranger had miraculously appeared on her doorstep and made it possible for her to keep the home in which she had lived since childhood.

Chapter 22

With his hands wedged in his pants pockets, King wore a meditative expression as he rode an elevator to the top floor of a five-star hotel.

Walking down a carpeted hall, he stopped before room 334 and knocked. Several seconds passed before the door was opened by a robe-wearing Unique, who stepped aside for him to enter.

After three long and miserable days of being separated from her, King had reached out and asked if they could talk.

"That's what we doing right now, ain't it?" she had sassily replied.

He insisted it be done in person, to which she reluctantly agreed.

"So, what can I do for you?" Unique icily inquired, with her hands on her hips.

Recalling his rehearsed spiel, he first explained he had never doubted her credibility and apologized that it appeared that way. "I ain't never loved nobody the way I do you. I've told you my situation, so you know how much I enjoy feeling a woman's love and affection. I know some people might call it a weakness, but I call it a need. And I can't help it. So, for me to have met a woman like you, who don't judge me or look down on me for that, I appreciate you more than you could ever imagine. And I just can't see me giving you up... at least not without a fight."

King then went on to address her comment in regard to only being concerned about his and her well-being. "You entitled to your feelings, and I understand that. And I appreciate your concern about me. But I need you to also understand that Double-O is my only friend, and vice versa. I know he a lil' standoffish, but that nigga gotta good heart for real. And he'd protect your life just as fiercely as he would mines. So, while I'll always put you first, please don't make me choose between y'all. And when it's time for us to relocate, I promise it'll be just me and you."

Now wearing a softer expression, Unique looked at him with a slight grin, "King, did I hear you say you love me?"

Nodding his head, he confessed he had been in love with her for a while now. "I ain't never told a girl that before, so I really didn't know how to bring it up. Plus, I ain't gon' lie, I was lightweight scared you might not say it back."

"Yeah, well, I also gotta confession to make. I've been feeling the exact same way. But I was just waiting on your scary-ass to say something."

"Why I gotta be the scary one?" King laughed. "When you was just as scared."

"Because you the man, King. So, that means you're supposed to take the lead. Duhhh."

Grabbing Unique by the front of her robe, he pulled her to him and initiated a deep kiss.

"What was that?" she huskily breathed in between a brief break.

"Me taking the lead," he answered before recapturing her soft lips.

Without breaking the kiss as she led him across the room, Unique pushed him down onto the sofa and straddled his lap. "I want to have all your babies," she whispered in his ear.

"What's up with that stick?" he asked, referring to the pregnancy test she had thrown on the floor the other day.

"Didn't you look at it?"

"Clearly."

"Then you already know the answer. I'm pregnant, daddy."

King closed his eyes in elation. And he didn't care about the gender, only that the baby be brought up by both parents. And he'd do everything within his means to ensure his seed received the love and affection he had longed for during his own childhood.

"We gotta start putting up money," he advised her, already thinking ahead. "So, when you doing the count, I want you to start setting something aside for the baby."

Unique nodded, "Yeah, we definitely on the same page, daddy. Because until we completely done with the streets, our lives are in constant danger. So, if something was to ever happen, the last thing I would want is for our baby to grow up struggling. We did enough of that on our own."

On account of the mood, King thought about something and knew it was the right time to ask. "Baby, why you never talk about your childhood, or family? It couldn't have been no worse than mine."

Her eyes adopted a reflective expression, as if she was recalling bitter scenes of a sorrowful story. Then, after a long moment, she looked down and truthfully answered, "My childhood was rough, both mentally and physically. And I don't speak on my family because I never knew 'em. My mama gave me up, and I was raised by the state. I was put in different foster homes and abused by different men. Then I got adopted by a woman in Flint. And she was Pee-Wee's aunt, which is how he came to be my cousin. And that's my story. I don't talk about it, because what's the point in bringing up a bunch of bad memories?"

Touched by her tragic tale, King protectively pulled her into his arms. "I'm sorry to hear that, love. But we ain't gotta worry about being mistreated no more. And now we get to start our own family."

"I appreciate that. But there's no need to be sorry, King. We don't get to choose our parents, or the circumstances of our childhood. It's life. And besides, there's others who have had it much worse."

She grabbed his face in both hands, "But you know what we do get to choose?"

"What?"

"Our child's future. We can make sure they never go through what we did. So, daddy, it's time to really run this bag up, and get the fuck out of dodge."

In total agreement, he nodded, "Yeah, you right. So, let's get back to it, then."

"First things first," Unique said, then slid off his lap and onto the floor. "Because I've been dehydrated for three days. And I need something to drink."

As she unfastened his pants and bobbed her head at a turtle's pace, King closed his eyes and surrendered to the marvelous feeling of her magical mouth.

***

With King behind the wheel, he and Unique were travelling through traffic in her sky-blue Range Rover. En route to a beauty salon, they were about to meet up with the white girl, Paris, for another supply of Fentanyl. This time, however, they'd be purchasing two kilos.

As King turned into the salon and put the Rover's back end to the building, the red Durango followed suit. Behind its tinted windows were Double-O and CJ, who were there to oversee the quarter-million-dollar transaction.

Nearly ten minutes late, Paris pulled into the parking lot in a green car that was noisier than a children's playground.

The plan had been for Unique to join her inside her car and exchange purses like last time, but instinct persuaded Unique to do otherwise. So, she lowered her window, stuck her arm out and waved for Paris to join her instead.

When Paris exited the car in clothing that clashed with her standard appearance, warning flags instantly rose in Unique's mind.

"Is it me, or do this bitch look bad?"

"Compared to last time, she do," King shrugged, "But maybe this her way of playing it off. Because she damn sure don't look like she got two bricks of fetty on her."

Paris climbed in the backseat and flashed a nervous smile. "Hey, girl, is everything cool? Because I thought you was supposed to get in with me."

"Nah, we good. I twisted my ankle this morning, that's all."

"Oh… Ok," Paris said, sniffling. "Well, Rico waiting on me, and you know how I get when I take too long."

As Paris passed her purse up front, Unique eyed it as if it might be infected with a deadly disease. "Damn, bitch, you ain't got that nineteen, do you?"

"Nineteen?" Paris asked, genuinely confused.

"Covid, bitch. You ain't sick, is you?"

"Of course not. Why would you think that?"

"Because you keep sniffling and shit."

Paris waved her off with a smile, "Nah, girl, that's just my allergies acting up."

Accepting the purse in reluctance, Unique peered inside at two perfectly wrapped packages. "Let your dude know it's about time for him to meet my dude," she said, passing her purse to Paris. "Because with the amount of money we spending, they need to negotiate some better prices."

"Alright, I will," she replied, halfway out the door. "And y'all take care."

As Paris was scurrying toward her car, Unique removed one of the packages from the purse. She could immediately tell by its weight that something was wrong. Foregoing delicacy, she used a key to slice an opening in the package and brought it up to her nose.

"This shit baking soda!" she exclaimed before hopping out the truck.

Inside her car, Paris was in a state of panic as it failed to start. When she looked up and saw Unique running across the parking lot on an uninjured ankle, she hurriedly reached to lock all her doors.

"Open this fucking door, bitch!" Unique screamed, banging on the window.

As Paris resumed frantically turning the ignition, Unique untied her Gucci scarf, wrapped it around her hand and shattered the window with a right cross.

"Bitch, you tried to play me!" she snarled, dragging Paris out the car by her hair.

Unique was using her knees and feet to teach Paris a painful lesson, when King and Double-O ran up.

"Come on, girl, chill out," King said, as he grabbed Unique around the waist and lifted her up. "You gon' fuck around and kill this bitch. And think about the baby."

When Double-O reached in the car to grab the money, Unique told him to grab Paris' phone as well. In spite of her anger, her brain was still on business.

As they sped out of the parking lot leaving Paris unconscious, lying on the ground, Unique scrolled through the girl's phone until she came across the name "Rico." Using her own phone to dial his number on speaker and he picked up after several rings.

"Hello?" he answered in a mildly curious tone.

"Yeah, this Unique. I don't know if you remember me, but we met—"

"Yeah, yeah, yeah, I remember," he quickly cut her off. "What's going on?"

"Not to be all in your business, but is you still rocking with old girl?"

"Nah, shorty picked up habits I don't approve of."

"Yeah, I figured that. But listen, do your people still be having them purses for sale? Because I was trying to get like two of 'em."

Rico chuckled. "I bet old girl tried to bang you some fake ones, huh?"

"You already know. But I ain't going."

Rico gave her the name of a convenience store and said to meet him there in two hours. "And I'ma make sure you get the same official joints as last time."

As Unique disconnected the call, King shook his head at her and smiled.

"What?" she asked, taking on an innocent expression.

"Girl, you something else. You out here whooping bitches and conducting business at the same damn time."

She leaned over to peck his lips. "That's because I don't play when it come to my daddy. Seeing you succeed is the most important thing to me right now. And I won't allow nothing or nobody to interfere with that."

While her statement was uttered in absolute truth, her reason for pushing him toward the pinnacle of prosperity was propelled by a motive King wouldn't believe if he was told by Christ himself. The boy had a golden heart, and a naive mind.

And this would soon lead to his untimely downfall.

Chapter 23

Toledo, Ohio

Two tan Cadillac Escalades drove down Cherry Street, en route to a notorious neighborhood known as "X-Blocc." Behind the tinted windows of the lead SUV was Kavoni, who sat in the backseat, with Squeeze at his feet. Up front, Malloyd rode shotgun as Puma had the wheel. Upon their return to Detroit, they will either have won or lost a hundred fifty grand.

Turning onto Scottwood, Puma drove several blocks down and parked near a brown duplex. As she wedged Martha in her waistband and Malloyd grabbed a gallon of milk, Kavoni placed Squeeze on a leash, and they simultaneously exited the vehicle.

When Dolphin and three of his men emerged from the second SUV, you immediately noticed the collective appearance of everyone present, Detroit Lion tracksuits and N.F.L. chains crammed with colorful carats. The group was a sight to be seen as they marched in unison.

With Kavoni leading the way, they went around to the back of the building, where they came upon a pair of men in mainly blue clothing and matching ballcaps.

"What's craccin', Cuzz?" greeted the taller of the two, who had the stare of a wild animal.

"I'm here to scratch, my baby," Kavoni unblinkingly replied.

"Your baby?" he screwed his face up.

Kavoni smirked. "It's a Detroit thing, bro."

"Yeah, well, you in Toledo, Cuzz. And we big Crippin around here. So, save all that 'my baby' shit for Detroit, you feel me?"

Although forcing himself to stay calm, Kavoni envisioned himself withdrawing his weapon within a split second and turning this clown into a memory.

Before the situation could further escalate, Gipper, an older and more mature-looking man stepped out onto the back porch. He felt the tension as if it had physically touched him.

"What's going on out here?" he inquired of his two men, while taking in Kavoni and his team.

With his chin upturned, the wild one spoke, "We good, Unc. Cuzz just gotta fly-ass mouth, that's all."

Ignoring his nephew, Gipper nudged his head at the dog. "Who that right there?"

"This Squeeze," Kavoni answered.

Gipper smiled, rubbing his hands together in anticipation, "He here to see my boy, Hitler!" He extended his hand in invitation, "Y'all come on in. And don't mind my nephew, he don't mean no harm."

Once the last man with Kavoni passed through the doorway, Gipper addressed his nephew in a scolding tone. "Nigga, this fight worth a hundred-and-fifty G's. An if you had fucked this up, you know damn well you can't pay me half of that. You do that shit again, and I'ma forget you my sister's son."

Kavoni and his team were escorted to the gutted floor of the third story, where roughly two dozen people were in attendance for the highly anticipated match between Squeeze and Hitler.

When the crowd saw in surprise that Squeeze only had one eye, the majority began marking him off. But there was a person in particular who regarded Kavoni with a closer look. It was apparent from his appearance that he was a coin collector. And he had the seasoned, but savage stare of someone who'd stolen many souls. So, for him to wager seventy-five grand on a one-eyed dog, then clearly, he had a trick up his sleeve. As an opportunist, the man would keep these thoughts to himself and bet big on Squeeze.

Hanging from the ceiling in a corner was a hundred-pound scale with an attached harness. And placed in the center of the room was a sixteen-by-sixteen box in which the match would take place.

Before presenting his dog, Gipper had someone fetch a money counter. While Malloyd was widely known and respected throughout the dogfighting circuit, there was nothing wrong with ensuring the purse was not a penny short.

After a hundred-fifty grand ran through the counter, the money was given to the referee, who'd oversee the match. He was responsible for awarding the winner in the end.

Moments later, they heard heavy panting and the scratching sound of paws on the staircase. What soon came into view was an all-white Pitbull with a massive head and sinister eyes. Rippling with muscles, he bore facial scars that were indicative of his previous battles, all of which he'd won by unanimous decision.

Once the dogs were exchanged for cleaning purposes, Malloyd placed Hitler in a basin and performed his signature test of pouring milk over the animal. After allowing it to settle in the coat for several minutes, he ran his hand along Hitler's back and licked his palm. Unlike last time, when they'd been in Kentucky, there was no numbing sensation on Malloyd's tongue. So, he gave Kavoni the green light by way of a single nod.

After the dogs were returned to their owners, they were then led over to the scale to make weight, which was not to exceed forty-four pounds. A violation could result in a forfeiture fee, which in this case was seventy-five hundred.

When Squeeze was placed inside the harness and lifted in mid-air, he weighed in at forty-two and one-fourth pounds. However, Hitler barely made weight, without a pound to spare.

Now came the moment of truth.

Kavoni's heart was racing as they approached the box. Though he and Malloyd had done everything possible to prepare Squeeze for this match, there was still the fact that they were going up against a grand champ. But he was confident they could pull it off, as he and Squeeze shared an unusual connection that should work to their advantage.

Squatted alongside the box as Malloyd took Squeeze inside, Kavoni wanted to observe the action from the moment it began. As the owner, you could get within inches of your dog during the match but touching them was prohibited.

Inside the box, the referee stood in the center, while Malloyd and Gipper were in opposite corners, holding the dogs by the collar.

"Y'all ready?" the referee asked, looking both ways.

When they nodded in response, he yelled, "Release!" and jumped back.

Once the collars were snapped, Hitler and Squeeze fearlessly flew forward.

To Kavoni's dismay, Hitler's experience allowed him to lock his jaws over Squeeze's muzzle and began shaking him. If he didn't quickly get loose, the fight would be finished within minutes.

"Drive, Squeeze!" Kavoni barked. Having entertained every possible scenario, he knew a mouth-bite could happen and was prepared to defend it.

The crowd looked on in slight disbelief as Squeeze obediently followed his owner's command and began pushing Hitler around the box. What they didn't know, but would soon find out, was that Kavoni was capable of communicating tactical commands to his one-eyed canine. They had marked Squeeze off entirely too soon.

As Squeeze soundlessly drove forward, Hitler was twisting and rolling, while tucking his front legs in a defensive technique he'd been taught.

"I'm still here, boy," Kavoni assured Squeeze.

When his tail began wagging, Kavoni smiled, for that was a sure sign the dog was calm.

Kavoni began tapping the corner of the box where he was standing. "Bring him right here, Squeeze!"

No longer in slight disbelief, the crowd was now in amazement as they witnessed Squeeze force Hitler into the corner Kavoni had tapped.

On account of being placed in such an awkward position, Hitler released his hold.

"Now!" Kavoni barked, which caused Squeeze to sink his teeth into Hitler's exposed chest. "Big bites, Squeeze!"

Following orders, Squeeze opened his mouth wider and applied more pressure.

"Get him out of there!" Gipper yelled to Hitler. "Come on, boy, we been here before."

When Hitler attempted to return his jaws to Squeeze's muzzle, Kavoni ordered, "Shoot, Squeeze!"

There was an uproar of excitement as Squeeze lifted Hitler off all fours and slammed him back to the ground.

"Nigga, is you seeing this shit?" one man said to his friend in astonishment. "I ain't never seen or heard of no shit like this. But I should've known there was a trick to it when he brought that one-eyed mu'fucka up in here."

Because Squeeze's muzzle was bleeding profusely, Kavoni knew it was time to bring this match to a close so he could get him some medical attention.

When he called for Squeeze to finish the fight, his mouth instantly shot from Hitler's chest to his throat and locked on.

Knowing he'd been outwitted, Gipper instructed for the referee to stop the fight before his dog was killed. Despite his defeat, Hitler had won more money than he'd lost, which made his life worth saving.

As the referee approached the dogs with a stick used to break their bite, Kavoni put his arm out in obstruction. "You don't need that."

Once again, the crowd was in awe as Kavoni ordered Squeeze to release him and the dog immediately surrendered his hold.

"Nigga, I'm on your ass now!" Gipper smiled at Kavoni in good sportsmanship. "And I got something for his lil' one one-eyed-ass."

Giving Gipper a handshake and instructing Malloyd to grab the money, Kavoni scooped Squeeze up in his arms and hurriedly descended the staircase. Oblivious to the blood that was staining his clothes and jewelry, his only concern was helping his dog.

As they piled inside the Escalade, with Kavoni cradling Squeeze in his lap, he dug his phone out and called Mecca.

"Hello?"

"Aye, yo, where you at?"

"I'm at home," she answered, hearing the urgency in his tone. "Why, what's up?"

"Squeeze got hurt, and he need help."

"What do you mean he got hurt?"

"Man, why is you asking so many fucking questions?" Kavoni snapped. "Now is you gon' help, or what?"

"Of course, I'ma help. But you don't gotta be talking to me like that. Now tell me what's wrong with him."

He explained that his muzzle wouldn't stop bleeding, and his eyes held a strange look. "He looking like he real tired, or something."

"Don't let him go to sleep," Mecca warned. "And how long will it be before you get here?"

"I don't know, probably like fifteen more minutes."

The trip between Toledo and Detroit usually took around thirty to forty minutes. But with Puma driving like a bat out of hell, they'd cut that time nearly in half.

"Alright, I'll see you when you get here," Mecca said. "I gotta get some stuff set up. And make sure you keep him woke."

Disconnecting the call, Kavoni worriedly looked down at Squeeze and pled, "Don't fall asleep on me, Squeeze. I need you to stay up."

As Kavoni began to console him with loving words, Squeeze maintained eye contact the entire time. He loved his owner and had done everything he could to please him. Even when that other dog had hurt him real bad, he had refused to give up, for fear of disappointing the man who had rescued him from a life of solitude.

Mecca was standing outside when the Escalade drove up to her house. She covered her mouth in horror as a bloody Kavoni came running toward her with Squeeze in his arms.

In the basement, Mecca had set up a makeshift bed, which she instructed Kavoni to gently lay Squeeze on.

She was tenderly applying an ointment to his wound, when she noticed what appeared to be teeth marks. As her mind suddenly recalled the night when Kavoni had said the dog was on a diet, his strange and evasive behavior now made perfect sense.

After running an I.V. under the dog's skin to keep him hydrated, Mecca eyed Kavoni with a distasteful expression. "How could you?"

"How could I what?"

"Kavoni, I'm not dumb. I know you be fighting this dog. That's why you was acting all weird that one night. Talking about he on a diet and stuff. He wasn't on no damn diet. You was getting him ready for a fight."

Not knowing what to say, he guiltily averted his gaze.

"And do you even know the severity of his wound?" she imploringly asked. "The reason he wouldn't stop bleeding was because the other dog hit a 'bleeder' in his face. That's like a main artery. So luckily you were able to get him as quickly as you did, or he would've bled out."

Mecca shook her head in disgust. "I just don't understand how people can say they love an animal… but put its life in jeopardy."

"Man, it ain't even like that," he defensively stated.

"It ain't like that?" Mecca bitterly repeated. "Then tell me what it's like. Because I'm definitely all ears."

"It ain't no different than boxing," he explained. "You got fighters, and you got trainers. They set up matches, then they get in the ring and battle for the bread. It's just a sport."

Mecca scoffed at his logic and pointed out, "A boxer get hit, not bit. And that's a big difference. So, let's see if you'd like somebody biting all over your ass... since it's just a sport."

"Regardless of what you think, I got genuine love for this dog."

"Yeah, well, you gotta painful way of showing it."

Looking down at Squeeze as he took shallow breaths, Kavoni fearfully asked Mecca what were his chances of survival.

"It's too early to say. I mean, obviously he needs better medical attention than what I can provide. But I'll do everything I can. And the next twenty-four hours will determine a lot."

Interlocking his hands on top of his head, Kavoni gazed toward the ceiling and loudly exhaled in frustration. His dog was severely injured, and there was little he could do to help him.

"Look, why don't you go home and get cleaned up?" Mecca suggested. "I'll call off work tomorrow so I can stay here with him, and you can come back in the morning."

Appreciative of her assistance, Kavoni nodded in consent. And to him it was no coincidence that the woman who had nursed him back to life was now responsible for doing the same with his dog. As he'd known from the beginning, this was the woman with whom he was destined to spend the remainder of his life. And from this point forward, he'd go above and beyond in expressing the depth of his feelings.

Kavoni was shamefully leaving the basement, when Mecca called out, "Did he win?"

Flashing a subtle smile, he nodded.

"Yeah, well, I hope it was worth it." She smirked before turning back around.

After promising to sleep on his proposal, Mecca had discarded her better judgement and told Kavoni he had exactly one year to sever all ties with the streets. While she informed him anything beyond a relationship was temporarily out of the question, she did assure him they would be exclusive. But as she eyed Squeeze with a saddened expression, she wondered if she had made the mistake of committing herself to a monster.

Mecca laid down on the floor beside Squeeze and soothingly rubbed him. "Don't you give up on me, big boy. You've been fighting for survival your whole life. But mama here now. And I won't ever let him do this to you again."

Leaning over to kiss Squeeze on the forehead, Mecca continued to rub him as she began to softly sing a lullaby that was sung to her as a child.

Chapter 24

Inside May-May's apartment, she and Unique were engaged in an earnest conversation as they sat at the kitchen table. May-May was currently revealing her plan to go visit her family out in California.

"...Because this shit done got out of hand, girl," she worriedly continued. "So, I'ma just lay low for a while and let it die down. I already sent my daughter out there. Lord knows I'd never forgive myself if something was to happen to her on account of me."

"I hear you, May-May," Unique replied, "And I'm not trying to sound insensitive to your situation. But, bitch, you know what it was when you signed up."

May-May frowned in protest. "I didn't know they was gon' be doing all this killing. Do you see how many people dead behind this? Girl, they even killing kids and shit. And I'ma mother, so that shit hit different for me."

May-May lowered her head and sadly shook it. When she looked back up at Unique, there were tears in her eyes. "I knew Finesse wasn't never gon' leave his wife. And I know he wasn't the best man in the world. But, Unique, how I'm supposed to explain to my unborn child that I'm basically responsible for their father's death?"

It was actually May-May who was pregnant, not Unique. And Finesse had been the father of her unborn baby. When she gave Unique his phone number, she never imagined something so simple would subsequently lead to his demise. True, he'd been somewhat doubtful of whether or not the baby in her belly was of his DNA, but that didn't mean he deserved to die. Also blaming herself for the deaths of his wife and child, May-May knew if she didn't flee that city on the next thing smoking, she'd likely end up a patient inside the padded room of a mental hospital.

"Well, if you think leaving is what's best for you and your kids, then you gotta do what you gotta do," Unique said in support of May-May's decision. "But me, I'ma stay right here and keep running this bag up. So, if you find yourself in a jam out there, just call and I'll wire you that shit in a heartbeat."

May-May got up to wrap her arms around Unique. "Thank you for understanding, girl. And I hate to make it seem like I'm bailing out on you, but I gotta think about my daughter and the one in my belly. But if it wasn't for that, I'd stay right here with you and help you run it up."

Unique was leaving, when she paused in the doorway and offered to contribute to May-May's pocketbook. "Because Cali expensive, girl. So, you sure you don't need nothing?"

"Nah, I'm good," she replied, recalling how she'd saved the majority of her share from the robbery. "I should be straight until I can find a job somewhere."

"Well, alright," Unique said, hugging her in farewell. "You take care of yourself. And don't forget, all you gotta do is reach out if you need me."

After watching Unique disappear down the hall, May-May closed the door and leaned her back against it. Her plane was scheduled to take off in the morning and she couldn't wait.

"That girl dangerous," she smiled to herself before going to her room to finish packing.

Little did she know, the extent of Unique's danger would soon be unveiled.

***

"Higher, Daddy, higher!" Teeka joyfully cried as Dolphin was pushing her on the swing set.

Standing several feet away was the child's mother, Jada, who used her iPhone to record the father and daughter's backyard adventure.

Since the murder of Finesse's wife and son, Dolphin had been spending more time with his daughter. The gruesome killing had hit close to home, forcing him to realize his lease on life could be revoked at any given moment. So, until the day of his own demise, he intended to make as many memories with his daughter as possible.

As Teeka was now driving around the backyard in one of her Power Wheels, occasionally waving, Dolphin was watching her with a thoughtful expression.

"What's on your mind, baby daddy?" Jada asked, in genuine concern.

While they didn't always necessarily see eye-to-eye, Jada highly respected him for his outstanding support of her and their daughter. They'd been separated for over a year, but Dolphin still paid every bill and car note as if nothing had changed.

"I'm thinking about going to school," Dolphin softly answered. "If I don't get an education outside of these streets, I'ma end up failing as a father. Because I can't raise Teeka from a jail cell or a cemetery. But I don't know nothing besides hustling, so I either gotta learn, or risk leaving my lil' baby out here without a father."

Jada was both stunned and impressed. Stunned that he was willing to abandon a game she knew he utterly adored. And impressed by a decision she knew only a real man could make... placing his family above fortune.

"Kyrie, that's the most mature and unselfish thing I've ever heard you say," she complimented, addressing him by his government name.

She then reached over to grasp his hand in support. "I know how much you love that little girl. And I also know there's nothing you wouldn't do for her. But like you said, you can't help her if you're not here. So, I just want you to know you're making the right decision. And I'm here for you in whatever way you need me to be."

Teeka pulled up in her Power Wheel. "Daddy, you want to go for a ride?" she asked with a serious expression.

As both parents laughed, Dolphin replied, "Girl, don't you know I'll be done broke the shocks on that lil' thing."

"Daddy, this an Escalade," Teeka sassily replied before speeding off.

They were laughing at the liveliness of their daughter's character, when Dolphin received a call from Nooni. Dolphin knew it must've been urgent, with Nooni knowing he was spending time with his daughter.

Excusing himself, Dolphin walked out of earshot before taking the call. "What's good, bro?"

"It's about Butchy."

"Come get me," was Dolphin's immediate response.

Disconnecting the call, Dolphin turned to glance at Teeka, who happened to look over and wave. Though he hated to cut their afternoon short, Butchy had played an invaluable role in his life, which meant avenging the man's death was an obligation he couldn't forsake.

"Listen, I gotta make a quick run," he calmly informed Jada, "but I'm coming back. And I was thinking, maybe I could spend the night. It would be nice for Teeka to wake up to both parents."

Smiling at the thought, Jada agreed that was a great idea. "I can just her face now, when she wake up and see you still in the house."

Dolphin kissed Jada's cheek, then went to tell Teeka he'd be right back.

"But, Daddy, I don't want you to go."

"I have to, baby. But it'll just be for a little while."

He looked over his shoulder, as if checking to see if Jada could overhear their conversation, then turned back to Teeka and said in a secretive tone, "I'ma bring you a present back with me. But you can't say nothing to your mama about it."

Her eyes lit up at the mention of a present. "Oooh, what is it?"

"It's a surprise, girl. You just gotta wait till I get back."

"Ok, Daddy." She leaned up to give him a kiss. "But hurry back."

When Dolphin paused on the patio to peer back at Teeka, she was watching him with an intensity that gave him chills. As if burning his features into the core of her memory, it's like the little girl knew this was the last time she'd ever see her father alive.

Chapter 25

Unique was on her way home, when she thought she picked up on a tail. It was a dark-colored SUV that had been behind her for a suspicious amount of time.

When she made a sudden turn at the next street, the SUV soon appeared in her rearview. Involved in a number of unlawful affairs, she knew it could only be law enforcement or lawless extortionists. Either way, it was bad for business.

As Unique was calmly considering her next best move, the SUV sped around her and slammed on its brakes, forcing her to follow suit.

Before she could throw the Range in reverse, a masked figure hopped out the SUV's backseat. Clutching some sort of an assault rifle, he barked for Unique to exit the truck or be executed.

With only a split second to think, she slyly dialed a number on her phone and slipped it inside her purse. Then, placing her vehicle in park, she took a deep breath and followed the gunman's instructions.

After she was forced to lie face down on the floor of the backseat, the SUV sped off into the night.

"I'ma ask you some questions," Dolphin spoke from up front in the passenger seat. "And one lie will cost you your whole life. And my lil' youngin back there with you is fried, so you can only imagine what he gon' take you through."

His first question was whether or not she was a bartender at the gambling joint where Butchy had been killed during the deadly robbery.

Unique hesitated a brief second before nodding her head into the floor. He clearly had her confused with someone else, so she instinctively decided it was best to keep her identity a secret.

Dolphin's very next question made her grateful for doing so.

"You know a bitch named Unique?"

Again, Unique nodded.

What she didn't know was that they had watched her leave May-May's apartment. And since neither man had ever seen, or personally knew Unique, they assumed it was May-May who climbed in the sky-blue Range Rover. So, this was actually a case of mistaken identity that could work in Unique's favor.

"This next question is real crucial," Dolphin continued, "So, you might want to make sure you tell me the truth. Because I'm only gon' ask it once. Now, tell me if that bitch, Unique, used you to set that robbery up at your job."

After hardly a moment's hesitation, she truthfully nodded. "But she didn't say nothing about nobody getting killed, though. I swear."

"Who she have do it?"

"Her dude, King, and some nigga named Double-O."

Dolphin looked at Nooni, who was heatedly squeezing the wheel as he drove. And both men shared the same sinister thought... King was a homicide waiting to happen.

Dolphin and Nooni were reacting off information they had received from Puma. After Jazz had given her the name of one of Unique's associates, Puma had dug deeper and discovered a woman named May-May had indeed worked as a bartender at Unique's club, while also bartending at the gambling joint. Passing that information over to Nooni, Puma advised him that if they could convince May-May to talk, then surely they'd find out who was behind Butchy's murder. And, Kavoni's kidnapping, as they correctly suspected the same people were responsible for both attacks.

On a hunch, Dolphin asked his captive if she had ever heard the name Finesse.

At the mention of his name, Unique began quietly sobbing.

"Fuck is you crying for?"

In between sobs, she answered, "That's my baby daddy."

Dolphin frowned as if he hadn't heard her correctly. "Your baby daddy?"

She stuck a trembling hand in her purse and removed one of the two pregnancy tests she had stolen from May-May's house. The other stick had been used to deceive King.

"I'm six weeks pregnant," she cried, as Dolphin eyed the stick that indeed showed a "positive" sign. "I knew he would never leave

Keisha, but I still loved him. And they killed him over a dumb-ass phone."

"Who did?" Dolphin demanded.

"King."

She went on to explain how Finesse had confronted King at a barber shop about the theft of his phone number. After a gun was drawn by one of King's men, Finesse stood down, but vowed to attain revenge.

"He told me about what happened and I felt bad," she tearfully continued, "because I'm the one who gave Unique his number in the first place. But I didn't know what she was gon' do. And I begged him to tell you about it, and just let you take care of it. Because he used to always talk about you, and how you was like a big brother to him. But he said he wanted to handle it on his own. To show you he could step up if he had to. And now he gone."

As Dolphin listened to her convincing spiel, he felt a sense of sadness in knowing Finesse had died in an attempt to impress him.

"Bro, that's why they killed his son!" Nooni suddenly spoke up. "He knew the lil' nigga could point him out, and then it was only a matter of time before we found out."

Further enraged by the accuracy of Nooni's theory, Dolphin knew it was imperative that they track down Unique, who Puma ensured was the brains behind it all. He would make her squeal like a pig before pulling her plug.

"There's only one way I'ma let you live," Dolphin informed the woman he thought to be May-May. "And that's if you tell me where Unique at, right now."

"She at my house. Her and King got into it, and she been staying with me."

As Nooni made a U-turn in traffic and sped in the direction of the real May-May's house, Unique was pleased by a performance that could've won her an Oscar.

***

May-May was in her room, doing the last of her packing, when she heard a knock at the front door. Because she wasn't expecting company, she crept into the front room and peered through the peep hole.

Exhaling in relief at the sight of Unique, she opened the door. "Girl, you almost sc—"

Unique was shoved into the apartment and Dolphin and Nooni rushed in.

Before May-May could run, Nooni grabbed her by the hair and pressed a pistol to her head. "Bitch, I'll put a bullet in your shit if you so much as burp!"

Trembling in terror, May-May shot Unique a questioning look. As if asking, *why would you bring them here?*

"We gon' play a lil' game," Dolphin coldly announced. "It's called Q&A. I ask questions, and you give me answers. It's that simple."

When his first question was whether or not she knew King and Double-O, she glanced at Unique, wondering what answer she was supposed to give. But when Unique refused to meet her gaze, May-May reluctantly nodded in answer to his question.

"So, you know all about that robbery and murder they put down at that gambling spot?"

May-May's head dreadfully dropped. Thinking about her four-year-old daughter and the one in her stomach, she had known this day would come back to haunt her. But she had never intended for Butchy to die. She had only wanted some extra funds to better provide for her children. But regardless of her intentions, she understood karma was something unconcerned with excuses.

"I asked you if you know about that robbery!" Dolphin repeated.

May-May offered a subtle nod.

"I got one more question. And if you don't tell me what I want to hear, I'ma torture you till you do."

As Dolphin walked closer to May-May, Nooni snatched her head back so she was forced to look up.

Staring into her terrified eyes, Dolphin asked, "Where that nigga, King, at?"

A question she honestly couldn't answer, she looked at Unique with a pleading expression.

"Bitch, don't look at me!" Unique snapped. "You better tell them where that nigga at!"

May-May eyed Unique in confusion. King was her dude. So how was she supposed to tell them where he was? And then it dawned on her. *They got us mixed up. This bitch done told them she's me.*

May-May looked at Dolphin and declared in a desperate tone, "I don't know what she told you, but—"

Her sentence was severed by a sharp knock at the front door.

As everyone froze up like statues, Unique yelled, "Who is it?"

"Detroit Police, open up!"

After peering through the peephole, Unique turned back to Dolphin and nodded in confirmation.

Before he or Nooni were given a chance to think, the front door was kicked in and two masked gunmen moved in like SWAT. But instead of barking commands, they discharged bullets.

As Dolphin went down from rounds to his chest, Nooni died on his feet from a hollow through his cheek.

Leaving a trail of blood along the way, Dolphin was slowly crawling towards the back of the house. In a state of delirium, he was attempting to reach Teeka and offer his final goodbyes.

Dolphin yelped in pain as one of the gunmen brutally brought the bottom of his boot down on his back.

"Turn him over," Unique ordered before going to stand above Dolphin.

Coldly staring into his dying eyes, she shrewdly explained, "Like most niggas, you made the mistake of underestimating a woman. A black woman, at that. I'm Unique, silly-ass nigga!"

When she nudged her head for the gunmen to proceed, he bent to whisper something in Dolphin's ear, then stood upright and fired four rapid shots.

With her hand over her mouth to muffle her screams, May-May was appalled by the cruelty of Unique's conduct. The woman hadn't even flinched at the booming explosions.

When Unique spun on her heels and went to exit the apartment, May-May called out, "What about me?"

Unique turned back to face her with a callous expression. "We was only friends when the weather was good. Then soon as it started to rain a lil' bit, your scary ass was ready to fly clear across the country. So, I can only imagine what you'd do if they ever picked you up for questioning."

May-May placed a protective hand over her stomach. "But what about my baby?"

Unique flashed a devilish grin that would've frightened Freddy. "It's only six weeks."

When a gunshot rang out as she stepped into the hallway, Unique's heart harbored not a hair of remorse. She was a woman on a mission. And interference of any kind would not be tolerated.

As the gunmen led Unique to a dark-green pickup, they passed by the SUV Dolphin had left his soldier in to serve as lookout. While at first glance he appeared to be asleep, the blade of a Bowie knife was buried beneath his pulseless heart.

The trio piled inside a Ford Raptor, where the gunmen removed their masks to reveal the faces of Pee-Wee and his brother, Otha. They had been lying low in the city since the savage killing of Finesse's wife and son.

On account of King's sloppiness, which could've interfered with the completion of Unique's mission, she had called Pee-Wee and Otha in for a cleaning detail. However, when Pee-Wee showed reluctance in taking a child's life, the psychotic Otha had readily stepped up, saying it was no different than killing a fly.

As Pee-Wee put the Raptor in drive and pulled off, Unique barked from the backseat, "It took you niggas long enough!"

"Ni-Ni, you always complaining." Pee-Wee smiled, briefly looking over his shoulder. "I can hear you now, down in hell talking about how hot it is."

"Nigga, I ain't going to hell," Unique laughed. "Because ain't no way God want a bad bitch like me for an angel."

As they laughingly drove on, Unique thought of something and leaned forward. "Otha, what you whisper to that nigga?"

Smiling at the thought, he answered in a sinister tone that paired with his appearance. "Sleep tight... and don't let the bed bugs bite."

Fumiya Payne

Chapter 26

After the deaths of Nooni and Dolphin, for which Puma felt solely responsible, she was desperate to destroy Unique and all involved in her reign of terror.

"Bro, that bitch gotta go!" She banged her fist against the steering wheel, as she and Kavoni sat in the car. "She out here acting like she Griselda Blanco. Like Martha can't put a stop to that lil' shit."

"I hear you, Puma," he replied in a calm voice. "But we gotta be diplomatic with our moves."

"Diplomatic?" Puma repeated. "Nah, bro, we gotta fight fire with fire. Because this bitch all savagery, my baby. And if we don't match that shit, then I'm telling you, she gon' fuck around and have us in matching caskets."

"Puma, you know King more like a son than a brother to me. So, the love I got for him ain't the same as just two siblings. And girl, I don't want to have to end up killing my own flesh down. Regardless of what he's done, I know it wasn't intentional. Right now, he just blinded by what he think is love. And I can only hope he opens his eyes before it's too late."

While Puma could understand his line of reasoning, she still couldn't fathom the thought of allowing Unique to go unpunished.

"So, bro, how you suggesting we handle this, then?" she curiously inquired.

"I'm saying, at the end of the day, we still both alive and well. And our wins outweigh our losses. So why not make the wisest move and move around? Because I'd rather live on a farm in Wyoming, then to be buried in Detroit."

"Bro, I'm all with moving around. But this bitch ain't about to run me up out of my city. I can understand sparing King, but not her. She done put down too many foul plays to not get ejected."

"And what you think King gon' do when she come up dead, or missing?"

"You already said we can make it look like an accident."

"But he still gon' come unglued, either way. And I don't want that on my heart, Puma. You gotta remember, I made my mama a promise that I would watch over that lil' nigga. And she died giving birth to him. So, if I contribute to his downfall, then that means her death was in vain."

Puma accepted his statement as truth, but she knew it was provoked by something more than a promise to his mother. Because not long ago, he was prepared to punish King, Unique, and whoever else that played a part in his kidnapping. Kavoni's decision to forgo revenge was based on the same thing that had his younger brother in a blender, love.

Mecca had managed to capture his heart, which in turn had softened his savagery. And now that he was familiar with joyful feelings that were once unknown, he was becoming increasingly fearful of losing it. So, for the sake of something he believed to be destined, Puma knew her best friend was ready to surrender his weapon.

As Puma wore a thoughtful expression, Kavoni reached over to grasp her hand and confessed, "I think I might be in love, Puma. And I ain't even gon' sit here and act like I'm willing to just throw it all away. But from the bottom of my heart, I feel like everything that happened is my fault. And that's why I've become so slow to respond."

"But how can you blame yourself for any of this?"

"Because I crippled that lil' nigga when it came to character. I was so protective of him, that I didn't let him develop his own sense of identity. I did everything for him, instead of allowing him to learn certain things through experience. And now he older, he want to stand on his own, but he really don't know how. So, here come this woman who was able to sniff out his weaknesses. And to convince him she thorough, she got me out the way long enough to put him in a position even higher than the man who was allegedly holding him back. So now I'm the bad guy that tried to keep him in the dark, and she the angel that brought him into the light."

Puma had never thought about it like that, but it made perfect sense. Which made killing Unique all the more important. Because she was like a case of gangrene that required immediate removal before it could spread any further.

"So, that's why we really need to put this bitch to sleep, bro," Puma urged in a pleading tone. "We can't just let lil' bra fall victim to whatever game she playing."

"Puma, you literally like my sister from another mother. But I'm getting the fuck up out of here, my baby. I can't make you do nothing, but I can encourage you to use your reasoning so you can see ahead of the curve. And trying to save that lil' nigga right now is gon' cause everybody to drown. Self-preservation is one of mankind's most important rules. So, that means King gotta do what he feels in his best interests, and so do we. And I've decided to be one of the ones who live to tell about it. We gotta new plug, and more money than we know what to do with. So why not plant our flag somewhere else? Why run the risk of ending up like Al?"

Puma knew he was referring the movie *Heat*, which was one of their favorite bank-robbery films, starring Al Pacino and Val Kilmer. In the end, Pacino had gotten away with everything. But his hunger for revenge would not only cost him the woman he loved, but his very own life.

As Kavoni exited her car and climbed in his own, Puma offered an apology that he was unable to hear. Because despite his decision to decline the dish of revenge, Unique was a platter which Puma could already taste.

Fumiya Payne

Chapter 27

Hauling bags in both hands as they strolled through the mall, Kavoni and Mecca had just gone on a shopping spree. Despite it being his own birthday, he intended to make it a memorable event she'd never forget.

"I can't believe how much money you spent." Mecca smiled, looking down at her bags in disbelief. "This like my earnings for half the year."

"So, this all I gotta do to see that cute-ass dimple?" Kavoni teased her. "Because we can make this a weekend affair."

Mecca playfully bumped into him. "This ain't all you gotta do, mister. Because don't forget you still on punishment for what you took Squeeze through."

After calling off work for three days, Mecca had nursed Squeeze back to a full recovery. However, before allowing Kavoni to take him home, he first had to promise her that he would never subject Squeeze to such cruelty again.

As Kavoni and Mecca were leaving the mall, coming in their direction were two people who made Kavoni's heart start hammering.

Draped in designer attire and Cuban Links laced with twinkling diamonds, it was the sneering faces of King and Unique, who were trailed by a small entourage. She whispered something in his ear that caused him to look down at Mecca's shoes and chuckle.

"Look at my big bro!" King greeted, as he grinningly took in their shopping bags. "In here buying the mall up."

"Hopefully he bought that hoe some new shoes," Unique said under her breath, causing their crew to explode in laughter.

Kavoni clenched his jaw in anger. "You better put that dog on a leash," he warned King in a menacing tone.

"If a bad bitch like me a dog," Unique readily retorted, "Then what the fuck does that make that basic-ass bitch you got on your arms?"

Mecca sat her bags down and balled her little fists. "I ain't gon' be too many more of your bitches and hoes. So don't think I won't put these raggedy-ass Nike's all over your face."

Surprised, but proud of his girl's game reaction, Kavoni placed an arm in front of her to keep her at bay. "It's cool, love."

Unique scoffed in amusement, then looked at King, "Daddy, let's just do what we came to do. Because it ain't no secret this nigga jealous of you."

"Jealous?" Kavoni repeated with a contorted expression.

"Yeah, nigga, you heard me. You tried to keep him down, and now he's on a level where you forced to look up. The tail done became the head, and you can't stand it."

Kavoni turned to King and imploringly asked, "So, that's what you think, I'm jealous of my own lil' brother?"

King looked away and shrugged, "Man, it don't even matter, bra. I'm getting money regardless."

As Kavoni pinned him with an intense stare, Mecca touched his arm and suggested they just leave.

Ignoring her suggestion, he stepped closer to King and hissed in his ear, "Nigga, I bled for you. I still got scars from beatings you know you couldn't withstand. And you'll turn on me, of all people?"

Mecca used her elbow to gently nudge Kavoni along. "Come on, bae, let's get out of here."

"That nigga would've killed you if it wasn't for me!" Kavoni hurled over his shoulder. "So, don't you ever forget that!"

Kavoni was still trembling with rage as he sat in the passenger seat of Mecca's Honda. Of all accusations, he couldn't believe King would think he was jealous.

"I know you probably ain't trying to hear this right now," Mecca said before pulling off, "But I can tell your brother still got love for you. It was something in his expression. It's like he conflicted, or something. And from the way that girl act, I'll bet she's filling his head with all kinds of crazy thoughts. So, while I know you're mad at him right now, blame it on his mind and not his heart."

Nodding in acknowledgement of her opinion, Kavoni was reflecting on his and Puma's conversation from the other day. And the more he considered it, the more he realized she might've been right. Unique was unworthy of the mercy he'd been willing to extend.

As Mecca was steering them away from the mall, she glanced at Kavoni with a curious expression. "Bae, I don't mean to be all in your business. But what did you mean when you told your brother someone would've killed him had it not been for you?"

After several seconds of silence, she understandably inserted, "I'm sorry. I know you upset, so I shouldn't have even—"

"Nah, you good. It's just, when I think about everything me and that lil' nigga been through, I can't believe he would let anything come between us. And I hope you don't take this the wrong way, but what I was referring to was something I could never speak on. I shouldn't have even brought it up then, but I reacted out of emotion."

"No, it's cool, I totally understand. Because there's hurtful parts of my past that I don't care to talk about as well."

Angling his face toward his window as Mecca turned onto the interstate, Kavoni thought about King's failure to acknowledge his birthday. As he inattentively took in the passing scenery, his mind began to relive the December day that marked a pivotal moment in his life.

***

Flashback

It was customary for fourteen-year-old Kavoni to cut class early so he could pick King up from elementary. Their schools ten minutes apart, he would cover the distance in less than six.

Like clockwork, it was a quarter after three and children of various ages came racing outside. With King being quiet and withdrawn, he was usually among the last stragglers to exit the building. But after a long lapse of time between a student's departure, Kavoni grew concerned and marched toward the entrance.

Fumiya Payne

With his stomach in knots as he entered the building, Kavoni couldn't imagine what would be keeping King. This was something that had never occurred.

"Excuse me, young man, can I help you?" a male teacher questioned in caution. He had worked at the school for a number of years and knew with certainty Kavoni was not a student.

"Yeah, I'm here to pick up my little brother, but he never came out."

"What's his name and grade?"

"Kingdom McClain. And he in the third grade."

"Ah, that would be Mrs. Mathews. If you'll just wait right here, I'll see what I can find out."

Before entering the classroom, the teacher cut his eyes at Kavoni with a trace of suspicion. On account of the growing number of school-related shootings, paranoia was now priceless.

When the teacher returned to inform him that Kingdom had already been picked up by his father, Kavoni spun on his heels and took off running.

Having minimal contact with the eight-year-old boy, their father, David, openly exposed his hatred for King. So, to pick him up from school meant he could only be filled with two things, alcohol and evil intentions.

Breathlessly ascending the front porch of their house, Kavoni heard a scream that came from inside. Frantically trying to fit his key into the lock, he cursed in frustration at his trembling hands.

"King!" he called out upon bursting into the house.

He was racing upstairs, when another scream made him change directions and head for the basement.

The scene he saw as he descended the steps was like something out of a horror movie.

King was stark naked, and his head was clamped between the vise on their father's work bench. Crying, while uselessly trying to free his head from the device, he had bruises all over his back and buttocks.

154

With a Bible in one hand and a broken broom stick in the other, David drunkenly turned to face his eldest son. "Unless you want next, then I suggest you carry your ass back up them steps."

As he often did, Kavoni offered to accept his younger brother's punishment.

"Nah, not this time," David slurred, shaking his head. "Because see, I done figured out why your mama ain't here. She was too righteous to birth something this evil. This boy gotta bad demon in him, and I'ma beat it out."

When David raised the stick and brought it down across King's back, Kavoni charged him. He reached for the stick and tried to take it, but his adolescent strength was no match for a man's.

Maintaining his hold on the handle, David dropped the Bible and delivered a vicious backhand that knocked Kavoni to the floor. Then he made him curl up in pain from a kick to his stomach.

"Nigga, you must be done lost your rabbit-ass mind! Don't you ever try to take nothing out my muthafucking hand!"

As Kavoni cradled his stomach in agony, David resumed his beating of King.

Becoming enraged by his baby brother's piercing screams, Kavoni mustered up the strength to climb to his feet. But instead of attacking his father, he staggered upstairs.

Inside David's bedroom, Kavoni hurried to the closet and flicked on its light. Grabbing a shoe box from the top shelf, he lifted the lid to uncover a large revolver. Spellbound by its sparkling chrome, Kavoni picked up a .357 that had the weight of an infant.

Upon his return to the basement, David had the stick in midair, when Kavoni warned him to drop it.

When he whirled around, his eyes enlarged at the sight of the Magnum. But fear was replaced with boldness as he saw his son held the weapon in unsteady hands.

"Put the gun down," he coaxed, while edging closer. "I don't want you to hurt yourself."

Kavoni thumbed the hammer back. "The only person gon' get hurt is you, if you don't drop that stick and stop moving."

"You would really shoot your own father?"

"You would really abuse your own kids?"

"That nigga ain't no kid!" David angrily pointed at King. "He the devil. He killed your mother, for Christ sakes. Now give me that damn gun before I—"

David was blown backwards by a thunderous discharge. As he lay on the concrete, coughing up blood, Kavoni slowly approached him and the two locked eyes.

"The only devil I see is you," he coldly stated before firing two more rounds into his father's chest.

"Kavoni, help me!" King cried, snapping his brother out of his trance-like state.

Once his head was freed from the jaws of the device, King tearfully turned to embrace his big brother.

"You good now," Kavoni consoled him. *"And he'll never be able to hurt you again. But this a secret we can't ever tell nobody."*

Despite Kavoni wrapping the body in multiple blankets, a week later, the stench of their father's decomposing body became offensive.

Returning home from school one day, Kavoni and King entered the house and had to pinch their noses from the smell. Kavoni was no expert on decomposition, but he knew the odor would only get worse.

"King, I need you to go pack some of your favorite clothes in two bookbags."

"For what?"

"Because we gotta leave."

"Why?"

"That smell only gon' get worse. And it's only a matter of time before somebody else smell it. And I don't want to lose you."

"But where we gon' go?" King worriedly asked.

Kavoni shrugged before truthfully answering, *"I don't know. But it ain't gon' be here."*

As King went to go pack, Kavoni found a gas can down in the basement. After pouring a generous amount over his father's corpse, he splashed the rest throughout all three floors of the house.

With their backpacks in hand and their bodies bundled up, the two brothers stood at the back door and took one last look at their childhood home.

Kavoni then reached in his coat pocket and withdrew a lighter and one of David's favorite cigars.

"Burn in hell, Pops," he said in farewell before flicking the lit cigar onto a trail of gasoline.

Fumiya Payne

Chapter 28

After dropping their bags off at Mecca's house, Kavoni insisted that the festivities continue. "I'm not gon' let that lil' incident ruin our day. So, let's go get something to eat, and take it from there."

As they were having dinner and wine at an upscale restaurant, Mecca reached across the table to grab his hand. "I can't express how amazed I am by what you've done today. Because I've never known a man to splurge on his girl, when it was his own birthday. So, I just want you to know that I see you, and I'm thankful for having someone you in my life."

Kavoni nodded in appreciation. "Thank you, love. And I'm just as grateful to have a woman like you. Because I'm learning that a nigga can have all the money in the world, but he needs a strong anchor to hold him down. And for me, you that anchor, Mecca. I mean that. You motivate me to want to do and be better, and that's what I've been lacking. That balance. And that's why my birthday ain't all about me... but celebrating my better half as well."

It was women like Mecca who made Kavoni acknowledge and accept the powerful effect of having a solid partner. He now understood why in the corner of most successful men stood a strong woman. For what greater force was there than a man's strength paired with a woman's wisdom?

They were leaving the restaurant, when Mecca suggested they go to the movies.

Kavoni started smiling.

"What?" she asked, now smiling herself.

"Nah, it's just, I ain't never took a girl out to eat, then went to the movies. So, this like some real relationship type shit, you feel me?"

"But that's a good thing, right?"

He leaned down to kiss her. "Everything about this is good."

As Mecca was turning out of the restaurant's parking lot, Kavoni realized he didn't have his phone.

"Aye, yo, turn around real quick," he said while checking his pockets and the floor of the car. "I think I might've dropped my phone."

Coming up empty after a search of the restaurant, Kavoni asked her to swing back by her house. "Because I need to call Puma and have her go feed Squeeze."

"Here, you can just use my phone," Mecca offered.

"Yeah, that's cool, but I still need to find mines."

When they pulled up to her house, there was a shiny coupe in Mecca's usual parking space.

"Dammit!" she cursed in irritation. "I hate when people think that just because they gotta nice car, they can park it wherever they feel like it."

"Yeah, but how can you get mad at them, when they don't even know it's where you be parking at?" Kavoni reasoned. "I mean, it ain't like you got your name sprayed on the pavement."

Mecca eyed him with a scowl so raw that it made him raise his hands in apology. "My bad, yo. And you right. Muthafuckas need to be more mindful of where they parking."

Forced to park several houses down, Mecca slipped her house key off the ring and said she'd wait in the car.

"Girl, I know you ain't trying to see who come out and get in that car?"

"Would you just hurry up so we can be on our way? Please, sir."

"I'm saying, I saw how you flipped the switch on my brother's girl. So, I hope I don't come back out here and find you in the middle of the street, fighting over no damn parking space."

Laughing as the visual of it, Mecca playfully pushed him. "Boy, if you don't go find that damn phone."

On his way to her house, Kavoni looked around before veering toward the coupe in question. It was a late model Lexus the color of sand.

Peering through its passenger window, he noticed a woman's handbag on the seat. And to Kavoni's surprise, a car key protruded from the ignition.

"What you doing?" Mecca spoke from behind, causing him to nearly jump out of his skin.

"Girl, you can't be doing that. You damn near scared me to death."

"Yeah, well, if somebody come out here and see you looking all up in their car, you gon' be the one out here in the middle of the street."

"Man, I'm about to see what's in this bag."

As he reached for the door handle, Mecca grabbed his arm and nervously looked around. "Boy, if you don't come on!"

"Quit being so scary." He jerked his arm away. "Just be my eyes real quick. Ain't no telling what's in this damn bag."

Boldly opening the door, he leaned down and looked inside the bag. His eyes widened before he turned back to Mecca and urged, "Look!"

When she hesitantly peeked inside, she also couldn't believe what she was seeing. It was a Birkin bag full of cash.

Mecca tugged on his sleeve with a sense of urgency. "Come on, bae, we gotta get out of here. Anybody could be watching us right now. And they probably just waiting for us to try to take it. This a set-up."

"Hold up," he said, noticing a piece of paper sticking from under the bag.

Pulling it out, it was a Hallmark greeting card. And written inside was a message that he began to read out loud,

"Your eyes are hypnotic, and your smile brighter than the constellations above... your energy is angelic, as you possess an air of innocence like that of a dove's.

Your voice is harmonious, like a favorite melody I'd never grow tired of hearing... your laugh is infectious, and the loss of your friendship I find myself fearing.

Your love is abundant, its weight no scales could possibly measure... your loyalty is limitless, a quality for which you deserved to be treasured.

Your heart swells with compassion, despite emotional scars you bear from the past... your mind is intriguing, capable of performing the most difficult tasks.

Your mane is lustrous, long silken strands the color of coal... your kindness is notable, nosing its way into the depth of my soul.

Your nature is to nurture, providing joyful provisions that were once unknown... and if given the chance, I'd cherish you more than the most precious of stones."

After reading the poem, Kavoni pulled a speechless Mecca into his arms. "You like a precious stone to me, love. And now that you're mines, I promise to cherish you for as long as I'm alive."

As she just stared at him, still at a loss for words, Kavoni grabbed the Birkin bag and handed it to her. "This all you. Save it, blow it, it don't even matter. Because there's plenty more where it came from. But so that I'm a man of my word, make sure you give that girl, Tamra, something for finding me. Remember I told her I'd pay my medical bill."

A car door opened across the street and Puma unfolded herself from the slab's leather interior. She was responsible for the delivery of Mecca's lavish gifts. Gifts that she told Kavoni were a bit overboard.

"Look at the two lovebirds," Puma joked, as she walked up to greet Kavoni with a hug and Mecca with a handshake.

"I'm Puma," she said in introduction, staring directly into Mecca's eyes. This was their first time meeting, and she was just trying to get a feel for the thief who had stolen her best friend's heart.

"Trust me." Mecca smiled. "I know exactly who you are. And I've heard so much about you, I could probably pass a quiz."

Puma looked at Kavoni with an amused eye, then turned back to Mecca and asked, "When my birthday?"

"Nine months after his," she correctly answered. "So, you'll be twenty-five in August."

"Damn, bro," Puma playfully pushed him, "You have been over here running off at the mouth."

After exchanging several more minutes of light conversation, Puma excused herself. "I got Shawna in the car, and she gotta hair appointment at three. But, Mecca, it was nice meeting you, and I'ma see y'all later."

As Puma pulled off, Mecca commented with a smile, "She seem like a cool girl. And it's easily seen how close y'all are."

Kavoni nodded, "Yeah, that's a big part of my heart right there. She been down since day-one." He nudged his head at the Lexus. "And speaking of which, she the one who helped me take up your parking spot."

Mecca swatted his arm. "Boy, don't be getting me upset like that."

"I'm saying, no disrespect to the Honda, but you know I can't have my pretty lady out here pushing no bucket. So, I hope you like your new car. Bought and paid for. And don't think I'm trying to buy your love or affection. I'm just treating you according to how a queen is supposed to."

Slowly shaking her head in disbelief, Mecca replied, "Kavoni, I don't even really know what to say. Because I never imagined I'd be in a position like this. So right now, it seems unreal. Like an outer-body experience, or something. And then it's like, this was supposed to be your day, but you've managed to make it the best day of my whole life. Because this the stuff you see in movies."

"Mecca, the only thing I need you to say is that, as long as you see me trying to become a better man, you won't give up on me. You know, because loyalty is the most valuable asset a person can own. So, in return for mines, I'm only asking for yours."

"Remember the first time we met?" she said, smiling at the memory.

"Of course, I do."

"Well, the last thing I said to you that day was I already knew how your story ended. And it's true, the average street dude will end up in one of three places, a cage, a coffin, or a wheelchair. The numbers don't lie. But my point is, I could tell there was something different about you. Your demeanor, your delivery, just everything. And when I was driving off, I was wondering if it was possible to help somebody change their story's ending. So, while I didn't turn around, the fact that you came back into my life tells me it's no longer a time for wondering, but a time for doing. I also feel in my heart this is by design. So, to answer your question, yes. I'm willing to offer you my loyalty."

After sealing their pledge with a passionate kiss, Kavoni asked her to take him for a spin in her new car.

"I can't believe I'm driving a Lexus!" Mecca exclaimed, as she excitedly sped through the city.

"With a Birkin full of bread," Kavoni chimed in, holding the bag up.

"I ain't gon' lie, babe," Mecca reached over to squeeze his hand. "I've been struggling all my life. And it definitely feel good for the tables to turn. So, I just want to thank you from the bottom of my heart."

Later that night, as they were lying in bed watching an episode of *Love & Hip Hop*, Mecca told Kavoni to close his eyes.

When she had him reopen them, between her fingers was a men's gold ring with a cluster of small diamonds.

"This was my father's," she announced in a whisper. "And before him, his father's. So, it's been in my family for years." She looked up at Kavoni, "I've never given this ring to another man. But I know my father, and I know he would've approved of you. This is my birthday gift to you, as it's the closest thing to my heart."

When she slid it over the pinkie of his left hand, it was a perfect fit.

Kavoni pulled her into his arms and squeezed her. "Thank you, love. This the best gift you could've gave me. Because I know what it means to you."

While he didn't want to spoil the mood by bringing up the past, Kavoni was curious about the nature of her father's death. "I know it's probably the last thing you want to talk about, but how did your father end up passing?"

After a moment's hesitation, she began to softly reveal, "Like you, my father was also caught up in the streets. He tried to hide it, but I knew he was ruthless. But he was still my father, and I loved him no less. Then, eleven years ago, when I was fifteen, our door got kicked in by three men in masks. They drug me and my mother down to the living room, then made us watch as they executed him. And as they were leaving, one of them looked back at me and said, 'all vicious dogs are soon put down'. That statement stuck with me my whole life. And when I saw others in the streets suffer the same fate as my father, I knew it was true. And that's when I said I would never fall in love with someone in that life."

Kavoni now understood why she'd been so reluctant in allowing him access inside her heart. For her father had been slain in the same game in which he currently played.

"Damn, love, I'm sorry to hear that. Especially knowing that you went through something like that at such a young age. And my condolences to your father. But like I said, I'm preparing for my exit. Because the last thing I want to do is lose you or hurt you. So, I already know what I gotta do."

"Yeah, well, I'm telling you now. You pressured me into giving you my heart, so now that you have it, you better not break it. Or one us gon' do a life sentence."

Kavoni could see from her expression that she was as serious as a stroke.

"I gotta pee," Mecca said before climbing out of bed.

When she returned minutes later, Kavoni rose up in bed at the sight of her provocative image. In high heels, a lace bra and matching thong panties, Mecca stood in the doorway with her hands on her hips.

Instructing him to not to move, she cut on a song by Doja Cat and began lip-synching as she danced in tune with its melody.

"I can be your sugar when you fiending for that sweet spot/ Put me in your mouth, baby, and eat it until your teeth rot/ I can be your cherry, apple, pecan, or your key lime/ Baby, I got everything and so much more than she's got...

As he was given his first real glimpse of Mecca's frame, there was one word in particular that came to Kavoni's mind, flawless. She had beautiful brown breasts, a toned stomach, and a thin waist that flared out into rounded hips. When she turned to present the plump cheeks that devoured the string of her thong, he could only shake his head in amazement at the perfection of her symmetry.

Crawling onto the bed, Mecca drew his lips into a sensual kiss that fully awakened his manhood.

"I want you to have your way with me," she whispered in his ear, then tickled its lobe with the tip of her tongue.

Eager to oblige, Kavoni turned her over and trailed succulent kisses from her neck to her navel. As if her yoni was aware of what was in store, her legs mechanically opened at the closeness of his mouth.

"Ooh, I see somebody ready." He smiled, then rose from the bed and began to undress.

When he removed his briefs, Mecca's eyes widened at the sight of the snake-like organ that hung between his legs. "Damn, bae."

Smiling at her reaction while sheathing his serpent in latex, Kavoni remounted on the bed and began kissing his way from her feet upwards.

"Save the foreplay for later," she impatiently ordered. "I need to feel you inside of me right now!"

As he literally ripped off her thong and inserted himself into her virgin-like opening, she cried out in pain and clawed at his back. It had been a while since she'd been sexually active, and his size did nothing to help. But when they soon found their rhythm and the pain became pleasure, she encouraged him to go even deeper.

While fulfilling her wishes with depth-reaching strokes, Kavoni looked down and noticed that she was quietly crying.

"Baby, what's wrong?" he questioned in concern, slowing his pace.

"No, don't stop!" she protested, continuing to meet his thrusts. "I'm fine. I just never thought it would feel like this."

As Kavoni kissed away her tears and continued to patiently please her, he had no idea his world was on the verge of turning upside down.

Chapter 29

With rage in his eyes and a Ruger in his hand, King was standing in the center of his ransacked kitchen. Before him was an overturned stove, under which he had hidden over four hundred thousand dollars. And it was gone.

There was the sound of approaching footsteps, then seconds later, Unique came into view. Pausing in the doorway, she curiously took in King, the rummaged kitchen, then finally the stove.

"What the hell happened up in here?" she inquired, while continuing to survey the damage.

His chest heaving in anger as he stared at the floor, King didn't answer.

"Nigga, whatever it is, you ain't dead. Now tell me what the hell happened, so we can fix it."

He met her gaze with a murderous glare. "They took everything. All the money I put up is gone."

"How much was it?"

"Over four-hunnid."

"Babe, that's why they say never hide all your eggs in the same basket. But we ain't even gon' dwell on the mistake. We gon' figure out how to correct it. Because it's less than a handful who could've done it. So, did you rewind the cameras yet?"

He shook his head in disappointment. "Man, you know I ain't even been staying here like that. So, I forgot to even turn 'em on."

While King had failed to activate his, Unique hadn't failed to activate her own. Which is how she'd known where the money was hidden. Her game was coming to an end, and she was now making her few final moves.

She walked over to King and lifted his chin. "Look at me." When he complied, she continued, "We don't need no camera to show us what we already know."

"And what's that?"

"Let me ask you something. Besides me, who the closest people to you?"

"Double-O, my brother, and Puma."

"Exactly. Now, do you think Double-O would've done something like this?"

He shook his head without hesitation.

"And you know why?" Unique reasoned in agreement with his response. "Because all that nigga care about is you, and violence. In that order. So, that only leave two people."

"Yeah, I already thought about that. But I'm saying, they getting their own money, so why would they want to take mine?"

"Wake your naïve ass up, King! Can't you see this ain't about no money? This is all about him reclaiming ownership of you. Daddy, don't no big brother want to see his little brother outshining him. And when he saw you at the mall the other day, looking like you hit the fucking lottery, jealousy was chewing all through that nigga's heart. He can't stand to see you standing on your own. And that's why he would never put you in the game in the first place. And that's why he'll do whatever he can to put you back where he think you belong... in his fucking shadow."

The more he thought about it, the more believable her theory appeared. Kavoni wanted him back catching crumbs as they fell from the table's edge. He wanted him to return to the role of a lowly servant.

"Why this nigga think I won't bite?" King angrily barked at no one in particular.

Using reverse psychology, Unique gently touched his arm. "He still your brother, daddy. And I'm not saying he don't love you. He just feel you safer under his wing."

"Man, fuck all that!" He jerked his arm away. "That nigga can't just come in this bitch and take my shit. It don't matter who it is."

"But, daddy, I still got the money we've been saving for the baby. So, it ain't like we flat. We can just use some of that to get back on."

King eyed her as if she'd just accused him of rape. "So, what, you think I'm supposed to just let this nigga take over four hunnid thousand, and not do a muthafucking thang? Just chalk it up, and start over?"

"No, daddy—"

"Look, this what's about to happen. You gon' take your ass home. Then I'ma link up with this nigga and give him one chance to give me my shit back."

"But you acting like he just gon' admit to robbing you."

"You not hearing me, Unique!" King snapped, roughly grabbing her by the arm. "I'm not offering no other options. It's either he gon' give my shit back, or I'ma treat him like a fucking stranger. Flat out!"

She masked her inner joy with a worried expression. "Daddy, please be careful. And maybe you should take Double-O with you."

As expected, he heatedly rejected her suggestion. "Ain't gon' happen. I gotta stand up to this nigga on my own, once and for all."

***

While Mecca peacefully slept, Kavoni eased out of bed and began to quietly dress. As a result of Dolphin's death, he was forced to be more involved with the distribution of his drugs. But instead of working a phone, he dealt only in bulk-amount deals.

Kavoni was climbing in his car, when his phone began vibrating from an incoming call. Upon removing it from his pocket, he peered at the screen in surprise.

"What up, doe?" he greeted in a neutral tone.

"I'm trying to link up with you, my baby," King replied on the other end. "We need to talk."

"Alright, where you at?"

When King disclosed his location, Kavoni assured him he'd be there within the next twenty minutes. "Just let me stop at the gas station real quick."

Disconnecting the call, Kavoni was mildly elated by the possibility of reconciling with his little brother. Clueless of the actual motive behind King's request, Kavoni was prepared to swallow his pride and plead that they settle their differences.

Kavoni parked in front of the house he had helped King purchase and killed the engine. Mindful of the Magnum wedged in his waistband, he considered keeping it, then scolded himself for entertaining the thought.

"This my lil' bro," he mumbled, leaning over to lock the gun in the glovebox. Ascending the front porch, Kavoni knocked, and King yelled from inside, "It's open!" Surprise was the perfect adjective to describe Kavoni's reaction upon entering the house.

With his hand at his side, King was wielding a weapon that held thirty high-caliber rounds.

"Close the door," he ordered in an unfriendly tone.

Calmly complying, Kavoni inquired, "Damn, bro, what's all this about?"

"Me being the man you never thought I could be."

"King, miss me with the riddles and say what's on your chest?"

"Nigga, you think I'm playing!?" King growled, as he took a step closer and tightened his grip on the gun.

"Nah, nigga, I think you fooling!" Kavoni replied with an intense stare of his own. "How the fuck you pull a gun on your own flesh and blood?"

"The same way you came up in this bitch and took all my money!"

"Took your money?" Kavoni repeated. "First I was jealous, and now I'ma thief?"

"I didn't call you here to talk. Now, call your bitch and have her drop off what you took."

"And how much did I take?"

If defusing the situation meant compensating King for his alleged loss, then Kavoni would pay whatever number he named.

But King took the question in sarcasm and raised the Ruger. "Bro, I'm literally only giving you one chance to return my shit."

It was now clear to Kavoni that his brother was beyond reasoning. So, he resorted to what he knew best, survival.

Lifting his arms in a surrendering gesture, he inched closer to King as he earnestly pled, "Bro, I really don't know what you talking about. But on the strength that you my brother and I love you to death, I'll give you whatever it is you asking for. You just gotta tell me how much it is."

"It was over four-hunnid racks, nigga. You know what the fuck it was."

"Bro, on Mama's grave, I'll give you that. Money come and go, but family forever."

"I ain't trying to hear none of that shit. I'm done living in your shadow. I can stand on my own and you hate it. Now make the call and stop talking to me."

Kavoni looked at King in disbelief. "Is that really how you feel, bro? Or are those someone else's feelings?"

"How many times did I beg you to put me in the game? But you never would. Because as long as you was responsible for feeding me, you had control. But now I'm in my own lane, seeing in a week what you see in a month, and my big brother's pride can't take it."

Kavoni was now within several feet of the barrel.

"You got it all wrong, my baby," he informed King in a genuine tone of voice. "I've never wanted to control you or prevent you from becoming your own man. I just wanted to protect you. And that's what I've been doing since I was five years old, King. So, it's all I know. Just think about everything we've been through. We've been homeless, my baby. But did I not find a way to give you whatever you needed? Did I ever allow you to go to bed hungry at night? I killed our own father so you would be safe. And that was done out of genuine love. And love like that don't die off. You my whole heart, lil' nigga. And I'll give you every dime I got, if that's what it takes to make you see it's all love on my end."

Though King didn't respond or lower the gun, Kavoni could tell by his expression that his words were having an effect. And desperate to reach his heart, he asked, "Remember when everything got weird between you and Puma, and I stopped answering my phone?"

King offered a subtle nod.

"Well, that's because I got kidnapped, bro. They tortured me and left me for dead."

King's reaction strengthened Kavoni's conviction that he hadn't been involved.

"Yeah, bro," Kavoni nodded in confirmation. "They had Puma pay a hundred racks, and still tried to kill me."

"So, why you just now telling me all this?" King asked in suspicion.

"Just think about it. I get snatched up and removed from the picture, then your girl suddenly come up with a way for you to eat and a source to get it from."

King frowned. "So, what you saying?"

"I'm saying, she playing you, my baby. She had you in her sights from the moment she met you. I don't know what her end-game is, but I know she succeeded in getting me out the way long enough to turn us against each other. That's that divide and conquer."

Angered by his accusations, King snarled, "Nigga, she pregnant with my baby. That's the endgame. And she used her own money to put me in the position I'm in. So, with all the dirt you've done, ain't no telling who—"

Lunging forward with lightning speed, Kavoni slipped left and used his right hand to grab the barrel.

Several gunshots rang out as King reflexively squeezed the trigger.

As they were struggling for control of the gun, Kavoni managed to force the barrel downwards. "King, let go of the gun!"

"You let go!" he grunted, continuing to contend for control.

When King attempted to head-butt him, Kavoni jerked back and lost his footing. While falling backwards in what felt like slow motion, he heard the gun go off.

As they fell to the floor, with King on top, he stared at Kavoni through widened eyes. He opened his mouth to speak, but nothing came out.

"No! No! No!" Kavoni yelled, rolling King over to inspect his injury.

Gasping for breath, King wore a terrified expression as he gripped Kavoni's arms. "Don't let me die, bro."

When he raised King's shirt and saw the damage inflicted by the 40-caliber round, Kavoni knew it was bad. And with the bullet embedded somewhere in his belly, he also knew King wouldn't make it another five minutes.

As the two siblings shared the same sentimental stare as they had on the day of King's birth, Kavoni held him in his arms and shamelessly cried.

"I'm so sorry, my baby," he groaned in agony, rocking back and forth. "Please, forgive me..."

While incessantly whispering apologetic words, Kavoni felt King's body go limp in death. In a dreamlike state, he reached up to tenderly lower the lids of his lifeless eyes.

Gently laying King aside, Kavoni balled his hands into fists and bellowed in pain. He had just lost half of his heart, something nothing or no one could ever replace.

But little did he know, the pain had just begun.

Fumiya Payne

Chapter 30

One of the last cars to arrive, Mecca's Lexus coupe turned onto the cobblestone road of a cemetery and parked among a long line of cars.

Inside the coupe, a somber-faced Kavoni wedged twin Taurus semis in the waistband of his trousers. This was his first public appearance since King's death, and he was in no mood for tomfoolery.

After erasing his fingerprints from the weapon and interior of King's house, Kavoni had made an anonymous 911 call and reported what he presumed to be "shots fired" inside an east Detroit residence. He disconnected the call before questions could arise, then went home to Mecca and cried until his tear ducts were fully depleted.

The couple clad in dark-colored clothing, Kavoni and Mecca marched hand-in-hand toward the crowd who was gathered in attendance for King's burial.

People turned to curiously peer at the man who some claimed was responsible for his own sibling's demise. This came shortly after the newscast labeled his death a "robber gone bad," along with deceptive seeds planted by none other than the infamous Unique.

Feigning the role of a grieving widow, Unique was seated in the front row, flanked by a flock of felons who'd fire upon command. And among them was Double-O, who was eyeing Kavoni like a lion would a wounded gazelle.

With his eyes obscured behind dark shades, Kavoni stared straight ahead as he and Mecca approached the black and gold casket. As King's only immediate family, he had covered the entire cost of his funeral. Regardless of what anyone assumed, he loved his brother beyond description.

When an indistinct murmur came from somewhere in Unique's vicinity, Kavoni turned from the casket. Removing his shades to unveil a gaze colder than a parfait, he gave eye contact to the entire row.

"I came to pay my respects to my only brother," he unblinkingly announced. "But if one burial ain't enough, then we can arrange for plenty more."

As proof that he wasn't bluffing, he parted his suit coat to expose the dual handles of his handguns.

Rising from among the crowd was Puma, who was holding Martha in plain sight. She approached Kavoni and nudged her head at the casket. "Speak your peace, my baby."

With that said, Puma turned to keep a protective eye on the crowd.

Despite straining to hear, no one could make out a word of what Kavoni was saying to King as he hovered over the casket. They failed to realize he wasn't there to put on a theatrical performance, but to say farewell to a fellow he would mourn forever.

Leaning down to kiss King's forehead, Kavoni took one last look at his beloved brother and lowered the casket's lid.

Mecca clasped his hand and gave it a reassuring squeeze. Doing very little talking, but sufficient listening, she'd been holding and consoling Kavoni since the occurrence of the tragic incident. He had lost his only sibling, which meant it was senseless to offer an opinion on how to recover. Some wounds were to be mended on their own.

"I'm here if you need me," Puma assured, as she accompanied Kavoni to the car.

He nodded. "I already know. But just give me like a couple days. Because I do need to talk to you."

Before joining Mecca inside the car, Kavoni squeezed Puma in his arms. "You all the family I got left now. So, Lord knows I can't afford to lose you, too. That's why I want you to leave with me. I gotta few affairs to settle, then we can hit the highway, my baby." He released Puma and held her at arm's length. "Will you go with me?"

Puma smirked, "Bro, it ain't a place on earth I wouldn't go with you to. Just tell me when and where, and I'm there."

As Kavoni was sliding down into the coupe, Puma called out, "What we gon' about that snake?"

Knowing she was referring to Unique, he stated what sounded like music to Puma's ears, "Sever its head so it can never strike again."

***

As Puma was leaving the cemetery, she received a phone call from an unknown number.

"Hello?" she answered in a curious tone.

"Yes, this is Dr. Armstrong, over at Harper Hospital. Am I speaking with Shy'Ann Richardson?"

Puma frowned. "Yeah, this her."

"Ma'am, I'm here with your mother, Ms. Aretha Richardson, and she's requested to see you."

"Why she couldn't call?"

"I'm afraid her health won't allow it. So, if you have any desire to see her, I'd advise you to get here as quickly as possible."

Puma wore an irritated expression as she disconnected the call. She and Aretha hadn't spoken in several years. So, she was somewhat annoyed by her audacity to assume she should just come running to her bedside. And what was there to discuss, anyway? It wasn't as if Aretha wasn't responsible for the damaging experience that had altered the course of her life. Or as if she had ever attempted to offer anything even remotely close to...

"Ah, this bitch trying to apologize," Puma spoke aloud, as the reason behind her request dawned on her. "She done waited till she got on her death bed to want to get some shit off her chest."

Puma gave it some thought before deciding it was a trip she was unwilling to make. While we all made mistakes and were encouraged to repent, Aretha had betrayed her in a manner so vile, forgiveness could not be awarded. So, whatever demons she harbored would just have to accompany her to whatever realm she went to from here.

When Puma pulled her into her driveway and killed the engine, her thoughts were no longer on her mother, but on her and Shawna's future. As Kavoni's idea held promise and appeal, she could picture herself and the girl enjoying themselves in a new location. You can't subtract your past, but you can subtract the people and places that served as constant reminders.

Entering her house, Puma yelled Shawna's name before noticing a note on the living room table. She picked it up and read, "Puma, I'm walking to the store around the corner. Be right back. Shawna."

Puma cursed as she crumpled the note in irritation. There was simply too much going on right now for Shawna to be taking leisure strolls through the neighborhood.

Deciding she would go pick her up, Puma tensed up as she suddenly felt a presence behind her. With her hand reaching for Martha, she was knocked to the floor from a blow to her skull.

When she looked up and saw Unique, who was accompanied by two other malicious-looking men, Puma knew this was where her journey ended. Unafraid, she first thought of Shawna's safety, praying her assailants were gone before the girl's return. Then she thought of her beloved Kavoni. And at the thought of never seeing her best friend's face again, her heart was seized by a sharp pain that would outweigh whatever tortuous tactics her enemies had in store.

"And not that it matters," Unique casually stated, "But your girl Jazz was loyal. She wouldn't flip, and that's why I put that money in her luggage. I knew you'd suspect her. I'm just giving you a heads-up before you go see her."

Refusing to reward her adversaries with any symptoms of fear, Puma returned their stares with a stony expression.

"I've heard a lot about you." Pee-Wee smiled, as he reached down to remove the gun from her waist and toss it aside. "They say for a girl, your murder game impeccable."

Pee-Wee turned to Otha. "What you think about that, O?"

Eyeing Puma with the stare of a reptilian, he hissed, "I think we should treat her in accordance with her behavior... which is that of a man's."

"And I think you right," Pee-Wee replied before he put Puma to sleep with the butt of his pistol.

After bounding her wrists and ankles with duct tape, they wrapped Puma up in a blanket and hauled her outside to the trunk of their car.

Returning from the store with a bag full of goodies, Shawna would pay no attention to the green sedan as he casually cruised past.

***

Kavoni had been in a deep sleep, when his eyes suddenly blinked open. Now wide awake, he rose up in bed and discovered he was covered in sweat.

As he swung his legs out of bed, Mecca rolled over and tiredly moaned, "Bae, where you going?"

Slowly shaking his head, he answered, "Something ain't right."

"What do you mean?"

"I don't know. I can't explain it, I can just feel it."

"Come on, baby," she said, extending her hand, "Come back to bed."

Kavoni turned to face her. "I ain't going crazy, if that's what you thinking."

"Of course, that's not what I'm thinking. But it's two in the morning. So, I am thinking you might've had a bad dream. I went through the same thing when I lost my father. It's just one of the effects that comes along with tragic losses. And I'm sorry, baby, but you not immune to grief."

After taking a moment to consider her statement, he reached for his jeans. He withdrew a set of keys and removed one from the ring.

"Here, I want you to hold this," he said, holding it out to Mecca.

She eyed it in curiosity. "What's that for?"

"It's a key to my storage unit. It's where I hide my money."

Shaking her head, Mecca drew her hands back in refusal to accept the key. "Kavoni, I don't want that."

"Why not?"

"Because I know why you're offering it. And I don't want to even think like that."

"Mecca, listen to me. If something happen to me and Puma, at least I'll know you straight. I really care—"

"Well, let's just leave, Kavoni."

"We are."

"No, I mean right now, tonight. Let's just get on the road and go. If you really feel like something is wrong, then why wait around for something bad to happen?"

"I can't just leave Puma."

"Well, call her and tell her we're leaving. And if she ain't ready, then she can just meet us wherever we land."

"Baby, let's just wait till later in the day. Like you said, it's two in the morning. She already said she'll go, so we can be on the road by tonight."

Laying the key on the nightstand, Kavoni rejoined Mecca beneath the covers and held her in his arms. "I promise we'll be gone by tonight."

They'd been laying there in silence for several minutes, when Mecca softly asked, "You still up?"

He nodded, "Yeah, just thinking."

"About what?"

"About how this is all my fault."

"Baby, why would you say something like that?"

"Because it is. Me and Puma been knowing my brother's girl was poison. And instead of stopping her before it got out of control, I let her turn my own brother against me. But it's like, I knew he loved her, so I didn't know what to do. But instead of trying to spare his feelings, I should've been more concerned about sparing his life."

"But if that's the woman he loved, then what could you have done to stop her?"

"That's a question you might not want me to answer."

As he continued to lay there in deep thought, Kavoni couldn't shake the uneasy feeling he had in the pit of his stomach.

Chapter 31

After Puma's failure to answer or phone or return home by the following day, Shawna's worry had blossomed into full-blown fear. So, with no other logical alternative, she dialed the number Puma had given her in the event of an emergency.

When she had arrived home from the store the day before, Shawna was startled by the sight of Martha lying on the living room floor. For it was a mystery Puma went nowhere without her. But Shawna had decided to give it some time before pressing the panic button, a decision she'd soon come to regret.

"Hello?" Kavoni answered in an anxious tone.

"Kavoni, this Shawna."

"Yeah, what's going on? I've been trying to reach Puma all morning."

Shawna felt her heart drop. "I was hoping she was with you. She didn't come home last night. And she left Martha."

"She left Martha?" he repeated in alarm.

"On the living room floor."

"Shawna, listen to me," Kavoni said, as he began to hurriedly throw on clothes. "I want you to go to your room, lock your door, and hide till I get there. I'm on my way."

"Should I take Martha with me?"

"Absolutely. Now go hide."

After concealing a Glock beneath his jacket, Kavoni went to the bathroom, where Mecca was currently taking a shower.

"Aye, yo, I gotta make a run," he said, poking his head through the partially opened door. "I'll be right back."

She peeled the shower curtain back. "Where you going, bae?"

"I'ma shoot over to Puma's real quick."

"Alright, well, please be careful."

Kavoni paused by Mecca's bedroom and peered inside, where he briefly eyed the key as it lay on the nightstand. If he didn't make it back, at least she'd have a head start on whatever path she chose to pursue.

Descending the staircase, he was nearing the front door, when he felt the vibration of his phone. He exhaled in relief upon seeing it was a call from Puma.

"Girl, you had me worried like a muthafucka!" he answered.

"As you should be," came the reply of a man's voice.

"Who is this?" Kavoni demanded.

"It's ain't about who I am, it's more about where I am. Now turn your bitch-ass around. Slowly."

When following the caller's instructions, Kavoni found himself face-to-face with a tall, dark-skinned man he didn't recognize. And he was holding a sawed-off shotgun.

"That nigga you looking at," the caller warned, "will kill you quicker than Covid. So, if not for you, but for the sake of your girl's life, then I suggest you get on your knees and put your hands on top of your head. Slowly."

When he reluctantly complied, Otha walked over and delivered a beautiful roundhouse that rendered Kavoni unconscious.

***

When Kavoni awakened, his mouth was taped shut and he was tied to a chair in Mecca's basement.

"Well, well, well," Otha sang, as he and Pee-Wee stood before him with predatory glares. "It seems you and I have been reacquainted by fate."

Upon hearing his voice, Kavoni immediately recognized it as belonging to the man from the garage.

"One and the same." Otha smiled, as if able to read Kavoni's thoughts. "Now, shall we proceed with this evening's entertainment? Which I'm sure you'll enjoy."

Something began hissing near Kavoni's ear and he jerked his head away from the sound.

Exploding in laughter, Unique stepped from behind him and brought her face into view.

"My head still attached," she teased, then started flicking her tongue in a snake-like manner.

As Kavoni was eyeing her through pools of hatred, he could only dreadfully wonder what they had done to Mecca, who had been unsuspectingly taking a shower. And Puma... his beloved Puma. He prayed they had spared her of a prolonged death. Then he thought of young Shawna, who was still likely hiding somewhere in her room.

"You was a bad shepherd," Unique said, pointing her finger at him in accusation. "You let down everyone under your watch. And it's because of your failure that they're no longer here. In your narcissistic mind, you believed you could do whatever you wanted, to whoever you wanted. As if you could outrun or overpower karma. Stupid nigga."

The room grew quiet as the thudding sound of boots descended the basement steps.

Kavoni's heart was pounding in suspense. He'd murdered so many, that he couldn't begin to imagine who'd turn the corner.

As Unique and the others respectfully stepped aside, Kavoni couldn't restrain his shocked reaction.

Clad in a hoodie, fatigues, and unlaced Timberland boots, standing before Kavoni was a person named Mecca.

"Don't look so surprised," she said, clasping her hands behind her back. "Women have been outthinking men for centuries. You were just too arrogant to consider it."

After properly introducing Unique as her adoptive sister, and Pee-Wee and Otha as her first cousins, Mecca instructed for the tape to be removed from Kavoni's mouth.

"I don't expect you to beg," she said, "but I assume you're curious. So, here's your chance to cure it."

"Walmart," he growled, referring to the location of where they first met.

Mecca nodded, "I was following you. And when you went inside, I flattened my tire and waited. I needed to hear your voice to be sure it was you."

"So, from the moment we met, you was putting down a play?"

"I was." She again nodded. "And it took time and plenty of thinking. But I was determined to see this through. And only death could've stopped me."

When Kavoni considered the money they'd gotten from him during the kidnapping, plus the ransom Puma had paid, he was curious as to why she had allowed him to live.

Mecca smiled, "Because I couldn't find the money in your stash house. And two hundred thousand wasn't nearly enough to what I knew I could get. So, I had Otha spare you at the last minute. Then it was simply making it look like destiny had brought us back together. Because in order to get close to the money, I had to get close to your heart. So, the more I resisted, the harder you pushed. Because I knew when I did give in, the harder you'd fall."

"And look," she held up the storage key in triumph. "I allegedly gave you the key to my heart, and in return you gave me the key to your savings."

While Kavoni had once admired the accomplishments he'd acquired in the streets, he had to admit they were nothing in comparison to what Mecca had put down. She had rocked him to sleep in the gentlest of manners. And not once did he ever suspect it. He recalled once telling his old cellmate how he'd make the streets salute his savagery. But in reality, it was Mecca's savagery that was deserving of being saluted.

Not that it mattered at this point, but there was one last question Kavoni just had to ask. "Why me?"

Mecca exchanged the storage key for a phone and walked closer to Kavoni. She bent as if to kiss him but reached around to tug her father's ring from his finger. "You won't be needing this." After placing the ring in her pocket, she told Kavoni to listen closely, then played a phone recording.

"Bra, let's go!" was the sound of Puma's voice.

"Please, don't kill me," was the sound of a girl's voice.

"I can't kill what's already dead," was the sound of Kavoni's cold reply.

Boc! Boc! Two gunshots sounded off.

In spite of Kavoni's facial expression registering recognition, Mecca replayed the recording several times.

"Do you remember that night?" she asked, as a set of tears slid along her cheeks.

Kavoni slowly nodded. It was the night that had initially jumpstarted his prominent position in the drug game. With King being their driver, he and Puma had set fire to the back of a house and gunned down Chewy's henchman as they were forced to flee out the front door. They had been on the verge of leaving, when a young girl had exited the burning house in her undergarments. Kavoni now recalled the older model iPhone that had been lying near the girl's body.

"I was on the phone when you executed that baby," Mecca hissed through clenched teeth. "She had called me to come pick her up, when the shooting first started. I had her stay on the line while I was coming to get her. But when I got there, she was lying on the cold concrete in a pool of blood. You shot her in the back of her head. And I bet she never even saw your face. You just assumed you was killing some fucking junkie."

Mecca spit in his face and snarled, "But that junkie was my baby sister. So, you took something from me, and I took everything from you. I made sure you'll die without a dime to your name, or a loved one to attend your pitiful ass funeral. You will leave this earth as if you were never even on it." She flashed a wicked sneer and added, "You played the game, but I played it better."

As his mind involuntarily flashed back to their first sexual encounter, Kavoni now understood the cause of her tears. "When you cried that night, it wasn't from pleasure..."

"Not hardly," Mecca coldly concluded. "That was from the betrayal I felt from sleeping with the enemy!"

Fumiya Payne

Chapter 32

Kavoni didn't know how or when he'd lost consciousness, but upon regaining his senses, he was no longer in Mecca's basement, but in the driver's seat of his car. And it was surrounded by police officers, who were yelling for him to place his hands in plain sight.

As he attached his hands to the wheel and dazedly looked around, Kavoni realized he was in his own driveway.

"Now open your door, using one hand!" an officer ordered, "And slowly exit the vehicle."

When Kavoni complied, several officers rushed in and tackled him to the ground like he was a quarterback.

Once he was cuffed and stood up, a detective in plain clothes came to stand before him. "It's a pleasure to finally meet you, Kavoni McClain. I've been hearing a lot about you over the past few months. So, imagine my surprise when we get a call from neighbors, reporting what sounded like loud screams coming from inside your residence. You want to tell me what that was all about?"

"I couldn't tell you if I wanted to," Kavoni truthfully answered.

Just then, an unmarked squad car sped up to the house, and out jumped the detective's junior partner. "I got it right here!" he exclaimed, hurrying toward them with a freshly signed search warrant.

While they executed the warrant, Kavoni was placed in the backseat of a tinted Denali, where the officer up front warned him not to move a muscle.

When the canine unit arrived on scene, Kavoni knew this was another phase of Mecca's plan. And he could only imagine what drugs the dogs would detect. Let loose inside the house, the dogs would subsequently sniff out four kilos of raw Fentanyl, which was punishable by up to a life sentence in the Federal Bureau of Prisons.

"It looks like you're neck-deep in quicksand, McClain," the detective joked, as he opened the back door of the SUV. "And the feds are cracking down so hard on Fentanyl, that you'll likely be paroled from prison to a nursing home. So, on your ride downtown, you better—"

"Hey, Doug, come take a look at this!" an officer called out. When the detective went to peer inside the raised trunk of Kavoni's car, he couldn't believe his eyes. He turned to face Kavoni with a disturbed look before returning his attention to the small enclosure.

Curious to see what they were looking at, Kavoni lifted up in his seat and moved his head around for a better view.

"Sit your ass down and be still!" the officer up front barked. "Before you don't make it downtown."

Kavoni's curiosity would soon convert into dread, when a coroner's van drove up.

After huddling around the trunk for what seemed like an eternity, they removed a dead body from inside the small enclosure. Before they could cover the face with a white sheet, Kavoni caught a glimpse of the victim and nearly vomited. Having been shot twice in the head, with her throat cut from ear-to-ear, it was Puma's lifeless body lying on the gurney.

Without a morsel of shame, Kavoni broke down and openly wept. For his final memory of her would serve as a horrific image he'd never be able to erase. They had literally destroyed his best friend. And there was nothing he could do... but live with it.

As the detective retrieved two handguns and a large knife from the trunk, Kavoni was certain his prints would be present on all three items. In her cold and calculating plan, Mecca had ensured he'd spend the remainder of his life within the walls of a maximum-security prison.

Kavoni rode to the precinct with his mind in a whirlwind. While thinking he was someone with the ability to see several moves ahead of his opponent, he was actually just a lowly pawn in Mecca's masterful game. But unbeknownst to Kavoni, Mecca had one last piece to push before she would officially declare a checkmate.

Chapter 33

After being booked into the Wayne County Jail, Kavoni knew the chances of ever regaining his freedom were as likely as Jordan coming out of retirement.

Charged with capital murder, he lacked the funds to retain a suitable lawyer who could contest the number of felonies for which he'd been indicted. Needless to say, he'd be lucky to avoid a voyage to death row.

Once the ballistics to the firearms and knife came back, it was conclusively determined that all three weapons were used in connection with murders. While the knife and one of the firearms had been used to kill Puma, the other firearm was responsible for the deaths of Finesse, his wife, and nine-year-old son. And Kavoni's prints were lifted from all three weapons.

When King had made his confession to Unique and gave her the murder weapon, he had no idea he'd be sealing the fate of his own brother. Because after Unique presented the gun to Mecca, along with King's confession, it was Mecca who decided they would not only keep the gun, but also use it to finish what King had started. With the foresight to truly see several moves ahead, she'd seen the murder weapon would be instrumental in Kavoni's destruction.

To delay his death for as long as possible, Kavoni informed his public defender he wanted to cut a deal. Fighting four murders, with an overworked attorney who was approaching sixty, he knew there wasn't a juror in the country who wouldn't vote to convict.

"I'll see what they say," the lawyer had doubtfully replied. "But there was a kid involved. So, I can't make any promises."

A week later, the P.D. would return to Kavoni with disheartening news. "The prosecutor said the only way they're taking the death spec off the table is if you plea out to a life sentence, without the possibility of parole."

Choosing life over death, as he could always file an appeal or plan an escape, Kavoni agreed to the terms of their deal.

"Alrighty, then," the lawyer said as he rose to leave, "I'll head over to his office from here and notify him of your decision. And you should be back in court within the next few weeks."

Returned to his cell, Kavoni sat on his bunk and began to reflect over certain periods of his life for the thousandth time. And his thoughts always gravitated toward the same established fact, that he hadn't been in control. From the moment he pulled the trigger on that seventeen-year-old girl, the story was no longer about him, but all about Mecca's scheme to seize revenge. And what bothered him the most was he never saw it coming, which forced him to face his false sense of identity. Kavoni McClain was not who he had cracked himself up to be.

While wallowing in the misery of his miserable conditions, a guard paused at his door to deliver a piece of mail.

Wearing a puzzled expression as he accepted the envelope, the first thing Kavoni noticed was the lack of a return address. He tore it open and began to read.

"Death can sometimes serve as the easy way out. Because what suffering is there, if you're not alive to feel it? As I'm forced to go through life bearing the pain of my loss, it's only fair that you stand alongside me. We'll just continue our journeys from on opposite sides of the fence, lol. You were always so curious about the reflection of pain in my eyes. So, how does it feel to know you were the source of it?"

Instead of signing her name at the bottom of the page, Mecca left an impression of her lips in bright red. *The Kiss of Karma.*

As she had just made her final move and declared "checkmate," Kavoni came unraveled. Flying into a sudden fit of rage, he dismantled everything in his cell that wasn't nailed down. While screaming at the top of his lungs, he kicked the sink and toilet, until they were detached from the wall. He even hurled what little commissary he had onto the floor and stomped it.

Panting in exhaustion, a tearful Kavoni was seated on the floor in a corner of his room. As he was looking around at his imposed damage, his cell door slid open, and someone stepped inside.

When Kavoni looked up, it wasn't a guard standing over him, but a familiar face he had never expected to see.

"What's good, my baby?" Double-O greeted, gripping a large knife made out of fiberglass. "While you down there, you might as well say your prayers. Because this earth ain't big enough for the both of us."

Chapter 34

Amiri Marie Turner.

That was the name engraved on the tombstone that Mecca was standing over. With her hands wedged in the pockets of her peacoat, she was emotionally conversing with her baby sister.

"...and I don't think you'll ever know how much I miss you. Because there was nothing you could've done to make me love you less or turn my back on you. You had your struggles, but so do we all. And that's why I never judged you. Because unless I can figure out how to live forever, then I ain't different or better than anybody else..."

As Mecca continued to speak from her heart, she was suddenly joined by Unique, who quietly walked up and draped a supportive arm around her sister.

Unique's disclosure to King about her upbringing had been entirely true. She had indeed been abandoned and abused before finally finding a forever home with Mecca and her family. And because it was Mecca who had made it possible for the adoption to take place, there wasn't a favor in the world she wouldn't do for her big sister. Even if it meant deceiving a man she had secretly grown to love.

"...I know there's nothing I can do to bring you back," Mecca continued, "but I thought you might want to know I evened the score."

Unique shot her a look and Mecca laughed.

"Alright, I lied, Amiri," Mecca confessed with a smile. "I did a little more than even it. But just know that everything I did was done on your behalf. I love you, lil' girl. And hopefully now you can rest in peace."

As the two women were walking back to their respective cars, Unique glanced at Mecca and inquired about their future plans.

"Well, with all the money we got," Mecca smiled, grabbing Unique's hand and swinging their arms as if they were children. "I was thinking about a vacation. Somewhere nice and warm. What you think?"

"I'm thinking wherever you go, I'm right behind you."

"That's my girl." Mecca proudly beamed. "But for right now I'm thinking we should just go get something to eat. Because I'm starving."

Climbing inside her Lexus coupe, Mecca brought the engine to life and looked over at her passenger. "You ready?"

With a diamond choker enclosed around his neck, Squeeze answered his new owner with a series of joyful barks.

The End

An original poem is enclosed on the following page.

Sister Souljas...

We were enlisted in a war where our only weapon was will-power... but we've been equipped with the fact that beneath our helmets is the real power.

So, we laced up our boots of boldness and journeyed through a jungle of afflictions... where the land was littered with snakes of deception and fruits of addiction.

And though there were some who fell victim to vices that hindered... they eventually summoned the strength from their inner and refused to surrender.

I clearly recall the fear I first felt when deserted in the darkness of despair... and the stinging sensations from insects of envy that buzzed in the air.

I'm not ashamed to admit there was a point when I thirsted for a drink of affection... I shivered from the chill of rejection and began to view death as possibly a blessing.

Remember those nights when we cried as we crawled through the mud of depression? how we tiredly swam across the river of our tears with no sense of direction? or how the weight of our emptiness managed to diminish the desire for progression?

We howled for help, but it seemed as though no one could fathom our language... so we deemed it safer to suffer in silence and carefully sheltered our anguish.

Are we not souljas subjected to countless attacks against body and mind? have we not endured untold torture by those we once thought to be trusted allies?

But though bombs of betrayal have left our hearts marred with emotional scars... we are undoubtedly survivors by nature, and victory is ours!

A crisp salute to my Sister Souljas from all over the world. Chin up, feet forward

Yours truly,
Fumiya Payne.

Lock Down Publications and Ca$h Presents assisted
publishing packages.

BASIC PACKAGE $499
Editing
Cover Design
Formatting

UPGRADED PACKAGE $800
Typing
Editing
Cover Design
Formatting

ADVANCE PACKAGE $1,200
Typing
Editing
Cover Design
Formatting
Copyright registration
Proofreading
Upload book to Amazon

LDP SUPREME PACKAGE $1,500
Typing
Editing
Cover Design
Formatting
Copyright registration
Proofreading
Set up Amazon account
Upload book to Amazon
Advertise on LDP Amazon and Facebook page

***Other services available upon request. Additional charges may apply
Lock Down Publications
P.O. Box 944
Stockbridge, GA 30281-9998
Phone # 470 303-9761

Submission Guideline

Submit the first three chapters of your completed manuscript to ldpsubmissions@gmail.com, subject line: Your book's title. The manuscript must be in a .doc file and sent as an attachment. Document should be in Times New Roman, double spaced and in size 12 font. Also, provide your synopsis and full contact information. If sending multiple submissions, they must each be in a separate email.

Have a story but no way to send it electronically? You can still submit to LDP/Ca$h Presents. Send in the first three chapters, written or typed, of your completed manuscript to:

LDP: Submissions Dept
Po Box 944
Stockbridge, Ga 30281

DO NOT send original manuscript. Must be a duplicate.

Provide your synopsis and a cover letter containing your full contact information.

Thanks for considering LDP and Ca$h Presents.

NEW RELEASES

THE BLACK DIAMOND CARTEL by SAYNOMORE

THE BIRTH OF A GANGSTER 3 by DELMONT PLAYER

SALUTE MY SAVAGERY by FUMIYA PAYNE

BLOOD OF A BOSS **VI**

SHADOWS OF THE GAME II

TRAP BASTARD II

By **Askari**

LOYAL TO THE GAME **IV**

By **T.J. & Jelissa**

TRUE SAVAGE **VIII**

MIDNIGHT CARTEL IV

DOPE BOY MAGIC IV

CITY OF KINGZ III

NIGHTMARE ON SILENT AVE II

THE PLUG OF LIL MEXICO III

CLASSIC CITY II

By **Chris Green**

BLAST FOR ME **III**

A SAVAGE DOPEBOY III

CUTTHROAT MAFIA III

DUFFLE BAG CARTEL VII

HEARTLESS GOON VI

By **Ghost**

A HUSTLER'S DECEIT III

KILL ZONE II

BAE BELONGS TO ME III

TIL DEATH II

By **Aryanna**

KING OF THE TRAP III

By **T.J. Edwards**

GORILLAZ IN THE BAY V

3X KRAZY III

Fumiya Payne

STRAIGHT BEAST MODE III

De'Kari

KINGPIN KILLAZ IV

STREET KINGS III

PAID IN BLOOD III

CARTEL KILLAZ IV

DOPE GODS III

Hood Rich

SINS OF A HUSTLA II

ASAD

YAYO V

Bred In The Game 2

S. Allen

THE STREETS WILL TALK II

By Yolanda Moore

SON OF A DOPE FIEND III

HEAVEN GOT A GHETTO III

SKI MASK MONEY III

By Renta

LOYALTY AIN'T PROMISED III

By Keith Williams

I'M NOTHING WITHOUT HIS LOVE II

SINS OF A THUG II

TO THE THUG I LOVED BEFORE II

IN A HUSTLER I TRUST II

By Monet Dragun

QUIET MONEY IV

EXTENDED CLIP III

THUG LIFE IV

By **Trai'Quan**

Salute my Savagery 2

THE STREETS MADE ME IV

By **Larry D. Wright**

IF YOU CROSS ME ONCE III

ANGEL V

By **Anthony Fields**

THE STREETS WILL NEVER CLOSE IV

By **K'ajji**

HARD AND RUTHLESS III

KILLA KOUNTY IV

By **Khufu**

MONEY GAME III

By **Smoove Dolla**

JACK BOYS VS DOPE BOYS IV

A GANGSTA'S QUR'AN V

COKE GIRLZ II

COKE BOYS II

LIFE OF A SAVAGE V

CHI'RAQ GANGSTAS V

SOSA GANG IV

BRONX SAVAGES II

BODYMORE KINGPINS II

BLOOD OF A GOON II

By **Romell Tukes**

MURDA WAS THE CASE III

Elijah R. Freeman

AN UNFORESEEN LOVE IV

BABY, I'M WINTERTIME COLD III

By **Meesha**

QUEEN OF THE ZOO III

Fumiya Payne

By **Black Migo**
CONFESSIONS OF A JACKBOY III
By Nicholas Lock
KING KILLA II
By Vincent "Vitto" Holloway
BETRAYAL OF A THUG III
By Fre$h
THE BIRTH OF A GANGSTER IV
By Delmont Player
TREAL LOVE II
By Le'Monica Jackson
FOR THE LOVE OF BLOOD IV
By Jamel Mitchell
RAN OFF ON DA PLUG II
By Paper Boi Rari
HOOD CONSIGLIERE III
By Keese
PRETTY GIRLS DO NASTY THINGS II
By Nicole Goosby
LOVE IN THE TRENCHES II
By Corey Robinson
FOREVER GANGSTA III
By Adrian Dulan
THE COCAINE PRINCESS X
SUPER GREMLIN II
By King Rio
CRIME BOSS II
Playa Ray
LOYALTY IS EVERYTHING III
Molotti

Salute my Savagery 2

HERE TODAY GONE TOMORROW II
By Fly Rock
REAL G'S MOVE IN SILENCE II
By Von Diesel
GRIMEY WAYS IV
By Ray Vinci
BLOOD AND GAMES II
By King Dream
THE BLACK DIAMOND CARTEL II
By SayNoMore

<u>**Available Now**</u>

RESTRAINING ORDER **I & II**
By **CA$H & Coffee**
LOVE KNOWS NO BOUNDARIES **I II & III**
By **Coffee**
RAISED AS A GOON I, II, III & IV
BRED BY THE SLUMS I, II, III
BLAST FOR ME I & II
ROTTEN TO THE CORE I II III
A BRONX TALE I, II, III
DUFFLE BAG CARTEL I II III IV V VI
HEARTLESS GOON I II III IV V
A SAVAGE DOPEBOY I II

Fumiya Payne

DRUG LORDS I II III

CUTTHROAT MAFIA I II

KING OF THE TRENCHES

By **Ghost**

LAY IT DOWN **I & II**

LAST OF A DYING BREED I II

BLOOD STAINS OF A SHOTTA I & II III

By **Jamaica**

LOYAL TO THE GAME I II III

LIFE OF SIN I, II III

By **TJ & Jelissa**

BLOODY COMMAS I & II

SKI MASK CARTEL I II & III

KING OF NEW YORK I II,III IV V

RISE TO POWER I II III

COKE KINGS I II III IV V

BORN HEARTLESS I II III IV

KING OF THE TRAP I II

By **T.J. Edwards**

IF LOVING HIM IS WRONG...I & II

LOVE ME EVEN WHEN IT HURTS I II III

By **Jelissa**

WHEN THE STREETS CLAP BACK I & II III

THE HEART OF A SAVAGE I II III IV

MONEY MAFIA I II

LOYAL TO THE SOIL I II III

By **Jibril Williams**

A DISTINGUISHED THUG STOLE MY HEART I II & III

LOVE SHOULDN'T HURT I II III IV

RENEGADE BOYS I II III IV

206

PAID IN KARMA I II III
SAVAGE STORMS I II III
AN UNFORESEEN LOVE I II III
BABY, I'M WINTERTIME COLD I II
By **Meesha**
A GANGSTER'S CODE I &, II III
A GANGSTER'S SYN I II III
THE SAVAGE LIFE I II III
CHAINED TO THE STREETS I II III
BLOOD ON THE MONEY I II III
A GANGSTA'S PAIN I II III
By J-Blunt
PUSH IT TO THE LIMIT
By **Bre' Hayes**
BLOOD OF A BOSS **I, II, III, IV, V**
SHADOWS OF THE GAME
TRAP BASTARD
By **Askari**
THE STREETS BLEED MURDER **I, II & III**
THE HEART OF A GANGSTA I II& III
By **Jerry Jackson**
CUM FOR ME I II III IV V VI VII VIII
An **LDP Erotica Collaboration**
BRIDE OF A HUSTLA **I II & II**
THE FETTI GIRLS **I, II& III**
CORRUPTED BY A GANGSTA I, II III, IV
BLINDED BY HIS LOVE
THE PRICE YOU PAY FOR LOVE I, II ,III
DOPE GIRL MAGIC I II III
By **Destiny Skai**

Fumiya Payne

WHEN A GOOD GIRL GOES BAD
By **Adrienne**
THE COST OF LOYALTY I II III
By Kweli
A GANGSTER'S REVENGE **I II III & IV**
THE BOSS MAN'S DAUGHTERS I II III IV V
A SAVAGE LOVE **I & II**
BAE BELONGS TO ME I II
A HUSTLER'S DECEIT I, II, III
WHAT BAD BITCHES DO I, II, III
SOUL OF A MONSTER I II III
KILL ZONE
A DOPE BOY'S QUEEN I II III
TIL DEATH
By **Aryanna**
A KINGPIN'S AMBITON
A KINGPIN'S AMBITION **II**
I MURDER FOR THE DOUGH
By **Ambitious**
TRUE SAVAGE I II III IV V VI VII
DOPE BOY MAGIC I, II, III
MIDNIGHT CARTEL I II III
CITY OF KINGZ I II
NIGHTMARE ON SILENT AVE
THE PLUG OF LIL MEXICO I II
CLASSIC CITY
By **Chris Green**
A DOPEBOY'S PRAYER
By **Eddie "Wolf" Lee**
THE KING CARTEL **I, II & III**

208

Salute my Savagery 2

By **Frank Gresham**

THESE NIGGAS AIN'T LOYAL **I, II & III**

By **Nikki Tee**

GANGSTA SHYT **I II &III**

By **CATO**

THE ULTIMATE BETRAYAL

By **Phoenix**

BOSS'N UP **I , II & III**

By **Royal Nicole**

I LOVE YOU TO DEATH

By **Destiny J**

I RIDE FOR MY HITTA

I STILL RIDE FOR MY HITTA

By **Misty Holt**

LOVE & CHASIN' PAPER

By **Qay Crockett**

TO DIE IN VAIN

SINS OF A HUSTLA

By **ASAD**

BROOKLYN HUSTLAZ

By **Boogsy Morina**

BROOKLYN ON LOCK I & II

By **Sonovia**

GANGSTA CITY

By **Teddy Duke**

A DRUG KING AND HIS DIAMOND I & II III

A DOPEMAN'S RICHES

HER MAN, MINE'S TOO I, II

CASH MONEY HO'S

THE WIFEY I USED TO BE I II

Fumiya Payne

PRETTY GIRLS DO NASTY THINGS
By Nicole Goosby
TRAPHOUSE KING **I II & III**
KINGPIN KILLAZ I II III
STREET KINGS I II
PAID IN BLOOD **I II**
CARTEL KILLAZ I II III
DOPE GODS I II
By **Hood Rich**
LIPSTICK KILLAH **I, II, III**
CRIME OF PASSION I II & III
FRIEND OR FOE I II III
By **Mimi**
STEADY MOBBN' **I, II, III**
THE STREETS STAINED MY SOUL I II III
By **Marcellus Allen**
WHO SHOT YA **I, II, III**
SON OF A DOPE FIEND I II
HEAVEN GOT A GHETTO I II
SKI MASK MONEY I II
Renta
GORILLAZ IN THE BAY **I II III IV**
TEARS OF A GANGSTA I II
3X KRAZY I II
STRAIGHT BEAST MODE I II
DE'KARI
TRIGGADALE I II III
MURDAROBER WAS THE CASE I II
Elijah R. Freeman
GOD BLESS THE TRAPPERS I, II, III

Salute my Savagery 2

THESE SCANDALOUS STREETS I, II, III
FEAR MY GANGSTA I, II, III IV, V
THESE STREETS DON'T LOVE NOBODY I, II
BURY ME A G I, II, III, IV, V
A GANGSTA'S EMPIRE I, II, III, IV
THE DOPEMAN'S BODYGAURD I II
THE REALEST KILLAZ I II III
THE LAST OF THE OGS I II III
Tranay Adams
THE STREETS ARE CALLING
Duquie Wilson
MARRIED TO A BOSS I II III
By Destiny Skai & Chris Green
KINGZ OF THE GAME I II III IV V VI VII
CRIME BOSS
Playa Ray
SLAUGHTER GANG I II III
RUTHLESS HEART I II III
By Willie Slaughter
FUK SHYT   .
By Blakk Diamond
DON'T F#CK WITH MY HEART I II
By Linnea
ADDICTED TO THE DRAMA I II III
IN THE ARM OF HIS BOSS II
By Jamila
YAYO I II III IV
A SHOOTER'S AMBITION I II
BRED IN THE GAME
By S. Allen

211

Fumiya Payne

TRAP GOD I II III

RICH $AVAGE I II III

MONEY IN THE GRAVE I II III

By Martell Troublesome Bolden

FOREVER GANGSTA I II

GLOCKS ON SATIN SHEETS I II

By Adrian Dulan

TOE TAGZ I II III IV

LEVELS TO THIS SHYT I II

IT'S JUST ME AND YOU I II

By Ah'Million

KINGPIN DREAMS I II III

RAN OFF ON DA PLUG

By Paper Boi Rari

CONFESSIONS OF A GANGSTA I II III IV

CONFESSIONS OF A JACKBOY I II

By Nicholas Lock

I'M NOTHING WITHOUT HIS LOVE

SINS OF A THUG

TO THE THUG I LOVED BEFORE

A GANGSTA SAVED XMAS

IN A HUSTLER I TRUST

By Monet Dragun

CAUGHT UP IN THE LIFE I II III

THE STREETS NEVER LET GO I II III

By Robert Baptiste

NEW TO THE GAME I II III

MONEY, MURDER & MEMORIES I II III

By **Malik D. Rice**

LIFE OF A SAVAGE I II III IV

Salute my Savagery 2

A GANGSTA'S QUR'AN I II III IV

MURDA SEASON I II III

GANGLAND CARTEL I II III

CHI'RAQ GANGSTAS I II III IV

KILLERS ON ELM STREET I II III

JACK BOYZ N DA BRONX I II III

A DOPEBOY'S DREAM I II III

JACK BOYS VS DOPE BOYS I II III

COKE GIRLZ

COKE BOYS

SOSA GANG I II III

BRONX SAVAGES

BODYMORE KINGPINS

BLOOD OF A GOON

By Romell Tukes

LOYALTY AIN'T PROMISED I II

By Keith Williams

QUIET MONEY I II III

THUG LIFE I II III

EXTENDED CLIP I II

A GANGSTA'S PARADISE

By **Trai'Quan**

THE STREETS MADE ME I II III

By **Larry D. Wright**

THE ULTIMATE SACRIFICE I, II, III, IV, V, VI

KHADIFI

IF YOU CROSS ME ONCE I II

ANGEL I II III IV

IN THE BLINK OF AN EYE

By **Anthony Fields**

Fumiya Payne

THE LIFE OF A HOOD STAR

By Ca$h & Rashia Wilson

THE STREETS WILL NEVER CLOSE I II III

By K'ajji

CREAM I II III

THE STREETS WILL TALK

By Yolanda Moore

NIGHTMARES OF A HUSTLA I II III

BLOOD AND GAMES

By King Dream

CONCRETE KILLA I II III

VICIOUS LOYALTY I II III

By Kingpen

HARD AND RUTHLESS I II

MOB TOWN 251

THE BILLIONAIRE BENTLEYS I II III

REAL G'S MOVE IN SILENCE

By Von Diesel

GHOST MOB

Stilloan Robinson

MOB TIES I II III IV V VI

SOUL OF A HUSTLER, HEART OF A KILLER I II III

GORILLAZ IN THE TRENCHES I II III

THE BLACK DIAMOND CARTEL

By SayNoMore

BODYMORE MURDERLAND I II III

THE BIRTH OF A GANGSTER I II III

By Delmont Player

FOR THE LOVE OF A BOSS

By C. D. Blue

214

MOBBED UP I II III IV
THE BRICK MAN I II III IV V
THE COCAINE PRINCESS I II III IV V VI VII VIII IX
SUPER GREMLIN
By King Rio
KILLA KOUNTY I II III IV
By Khufu
MONEY GAME I II
By Smoove Dolla
A GANGSTA'S KARMA I II III
By FLAME
KING OF THE TRENCHES I II III
by **GHOST & TRANAY ADAMS**
QUEEN OF THE ZOO I II
By **Black Migo**
GRIMEY WAYS I II III
By Ray Vinci
XMAS WITH AN ATL SHOOTER
By Ca$h & Destiny Skai
KING KILLA
By Vincent "Vitto" Holloway
BETRAYAL OF A THUG I II
By Fre$h
THE MURDER QUEENS I II III
By Michael Gallon
TREAL LOVE
By Le'Monica Jackson
FOR THE LOVE OF BLOOD I II III
By Jamel Mitchell
HOOD CONSIGLIERE I II

By Keese

PROTÉGÉ OF A LEGEND I II III

LOVE IN THE TRENCHES

By Corey Robinson

BORN IN THE GRAVE I II III

By Self Made Tay

MOAN IN MY MOUTH

SANCTIFIED AND HORNY

By XTASY

TORN BETWEEN A GANGSTER AND A GENTLEMAN

By J-BLUNT & Miss Kim

LOYALTY IS EVERYTHING I II

Molotti

HERE TODAY GONE TOMORROW

By Fly Rock

PILLOW PRINCESS

By S. Hawkins

NAÏVE TO THE STREETS

WOMEN LIE MEN LIE I II III

GIRLS FALL LIKE DOMINOS

STACK BEFORE YOU SPURLGE

FIFTY SHADES OF SNOW I II III

By A. Roy Milligan

SALUTE MY SAVAGERY I II

By Fumiya Payne

<u>BOOKS BY LDP'S CEO, CA$H</u>

TRUST IN NO MAN

TRUST IN NO MAN 2

TRUST IN NO MAN 3

BONDED BY BLOOD

SHORTY GOT A THUG

THUGS CRY

THUGS CRY 2

THUGS CRY 3

TRUST NO BITCH

TRUST NO BITCH 2

TRUST NO BITCH 3

TIL MY CASKET DROPS

RESTRAINING ORDER

RESTRAINING ORDER 2

IN LOVE WITH A CONVICT

LIFE OF A HOOD STAR

XMAS WITH AN ATL SHOOTER

Fumiya Payne

Printed in the USA
CPSIA information can be obtained
at www.ICGtesting.com
LVHW010711010923
756909LV00002BA/213